HEADHUNTER

A WITH ME IN SEATTLE MAFIA NOVEL

KRISTEN PROBY

AMPERSAND PUBLISHING, INC.

Headhunter
A With Me In Seattle MAFIA Novel
By

Kristen Proby

HEADHUNTER

A With Me In Seattle MAFIA Novel

Kristen Proby

Cover Design: By Hang Le

Cover photo: Wander Aguiar

Paperback ISBN: 978-1-63350-083-9

For my husband, and his family, for introducing me to Victor, Colorado. I took liberties for this story, of course. But the heart of the town is here. I love you.

PROLOGUE

~IVIE~

"*I*'m not doing this for you anymore." I glare at my father and raise my chin, trying to appear way more confident than I feel.

My stomach pitches when he slowly turns to glare at me with cold, blue eyes. The same eyes that look back at me in the mirror.

But I'm nothing like the man who sired me. And I never will be.

Without another word, he turns back to the task at hand, making an egg sandwich. Our apartment is small and in a dirty little neighborhood in the Bronx. He says it helps us blend in, that no one will pay us any mind here.

In reality, he spends money as quickly as it lands in his pocket, and this is all he can afford.

I turn sixteen this summer, and he's already made it

1

clear that I'll be quitting school and taking a full-time job.

What I want doesn't matter. It never has with this man.

"Did you hear me?" I demand.

"I hear nothing important." His voice is calm, thick with that Bulgarian accent that I hate so much.

"I'm serious. I'm not doing your bidding anymore. If I get caught, I'll go to *jail.*"

"You are too young for jail."

"No." I shake my head and plant my hands on my hips. "I'm not too young. They'll send me to juvie. Either way, I'll be locked up, and I'm not doing that for you. This is ridiculous. Why can't you be a normal father instead of gambling and selling fake jewelry? Why don't you just get a real job so we can live a normal life?"

Without a look, he spins and backhands me, sending me sprawling on the floor. My cheek sings in pain, and I see stars as he leans over so close that his nose nudges mine.

"You are my *property*," he growls. "You are nothing but a female. And you'll do exactly as I say, *when* I say. If you try to defy me again, I'll sell you to the many men who have already asked for your body."

I gasp and stare up at him in utter shock and revulsion. "You *wouldn't.*"

"Yes." He stands and straightens his crisp, white shirt. "I would. Do not test me again, Laryssa."

2

The knock on the door is sharp, startling us both.

"I know you're in there, Pavlov," a man yells through the door, and all the blood drains from my father's face.

"How?" he whispers and then turns to me. "Hide me, daughter."

I shake my head, only enraging him further. He raises a hand, but before he can hit me for a second time, someone busts the door open, and three men walk inside.

"Did you think you could steal from us and get away with it?" The biggest one reaches for my father and pushes him against the wall.

This is it. This is my chance.

I scurry into my little bedroom and grab the bag I always keep packed—always ready to run if the opportunity arises.

I won't get another chance like this.

"No, I wouldn't steal from you. I just had to earn the money to repay you."

Another man punches him in the face as I slip out the front door and make a run for it.

My heart hammers in my chest. I can't hear the street noises through the rush of blood in my head and over my loud, panting breaths.

I have exactly four hundred and thirty-two dollars, some clothing, and my mother's wedding ring.

And a new freedom.

Because I'm *never* going back to live with a man who makes me do the things my father does.

I'll die first.

CHAPTER 1

~SHANE~

"*T*ake the shot."

The voice is calm in my ear, coming from several thousand miles away in a secure office at the White House.

I'm lying on my stomach on a rooftop, my sights trained on the target, but people keep walking in front of him.

"Not clear," I whisper and swear when the target walks into another room.

"It's taken three weeks for you to find him," the president reminds me. "Take him out. *Now.*"

Yeah, yeah. I don't need her to remind me how long I searched for this asshole. And as soon as he moves a little to the left...

I squeeze the trigger, and less than a second later, the target falls.

"Mission accomplished," I say and move quickly to the stairwell that leads to a waiting car below.

In less than three minutes, I'm safely away from the scene and headed to the airport.

"Good work," she says into my ear. "Now, get yourself home. The plane's waiting for you."

"Thank you, Madame President."

I nod to the driver, my partner for this operation, and he steps on the gas to get us to the airfield quicker.

Suddenly, the front window explodes, a bullet hitting the driver squarely in the forehead, killing him instantly.

"Miller's down," I say with a calm I don't feel as I reach over to take the wheel. I maneuver him out of the seat and manage to step on the gas, winding my way through the foreign city.

If I'm caught, I'll also be killed.

And I'm not ready to die today.

Only one car is following me, and it doesn't take me long to lose them.

"Your transport has been compromised," I hear in my ear. "The crew was killed. I need you to disappear for a couple of days. Lay low and await further instructions."

"Abandoning me in a foreign country wasn't part of the deal."

"We're not abandoning you," the president replies. "We'll get you out."

"See that you do."

~

"We expected you home a few days ago," my brother, Carmine, says as I walk into his office at our family's base of operations in Seattle, Washington. Rocco, my other brother, stares out the window but turns to look at me as I move farther in.

"Yeah, well, I got hung up."

I won't mention that I spent two nights curled up under a box, waiting for the US government to get me out of enemy territory after I assassinated one of the bad guys.

My brothers aren't allowed to know any of that.

It's better this way. The less they know, the less likely they could be killed for having the knowledge.

"Have I missed anything important?"

"Wedding plans," Rocco volunteers and then smiles at our brother sweetly. "I mean, it was a rough few days there, deciding between lilacs and freesia. And then there was the matter of the cake flavors."

My gaze bounces between Rocco—who's clearly getting a huge kick out of razzing our big brother—and Carmine, whose mouth firms into a hard line.

"He's the groom," I say simply and cross to the small kitchenette to see what kind of food we have stashed away in the fridge.

I'm fucking starving.

"I never pegged Nadia as the type to get all swept up in the fancy wedding deal," Rocco says thoughtfully.

"She's a woman," Carmine reminds him. "And big weddings are the mafia's way. You know that."

"So, which was it? Lilacs or freesia?" I ask as I return to the desk with a half-eaten sub sandwich and a bag of nacho chips.

"Both," Carmine says with a shrug. "She couldn't decide, so we went with both."

"As one does," Rocco says with a wink.

The door bursts open, and the bride-to-be herself hurries inside, her eyes wide with an emotion I rarely see on my brother's fiancée.

Fear.

"Carmine," she says as she hurries over. "I have Annika on the phone. She needs our help."

"Put her on speaker," I say, and we all lean in to hear what Nadia's cousin has to say.

"Okay, they can all hear you," Nadia says as she plants her hands on the desk. "Tell them *exactly* what you just told me."

"It's Ivie," Annika says, immediately getting my full and undivided attention. "She's been taken."

"Taken by *who*?" I ask, keeping my voice calm but feeling my blood erupt through my veins with a surge of new adrenaline.

"I don't know," she says and sniffs. "I got a call from her, but I was about to get in the shower, so I let it go to voicemail."

She sniffs again, frustrating me.

Just fucking *tell me*.

"I remembered it the next morning, *this* morning, so I listened to it. Oh my God, you guys. She's been taken. She was trying to get me to pick up, to listen, and help her. And I failed her horribly. I need you. Is Shane there?"

"I'm here."

"Thank God. Please, we need your help."

We all look at Rocco, who's already pulling his phone out of his pocket.

"The plane will be ready when we get to the airport."

"I THOUGHT Annika was going to tell me that this was all connected to Rich," Nadia says, shaking her head as the plane lands in Denver. "That there was more information or that someone else was dead. *Something.* I didn't expect her to tell me that Ivie had been taken."

I swallow hard, fear a very real and icy demon settling in my stomach.

I don't fear much. But Ivie and I have become friends over the past several months, and if my life weren't well and truly a shitshow, I'd take it much, much further with her.

If anyone touches a hair on her gorgeous head, I'll fucking skin them alive.

"Rich's organization fell," Carmine reminds his fiancée.

9

"We don't know that now," Nadia says, shaking her head. "Maybe this is tied to that. Maybe someone thinks they can get something out of Annika, or punish her by taking Ivie."

"We don't know what's going on," I remind everyone. "Let's get to Annika's place and figure things out."

My mind is racing. I haven't slept in seventy-two hours, and aside from the stale sandwich, I haven't eaten.

And I don't give a shit.

I need to find Ivie. Make sure she's safe and whole.

Annika's house is an hour from the airfield.

"You should sleep," Nadia says to me, her voice soothing. "I can see that whatever job you were on took a toll. You need rest if you're going to help Ivie."

"I'm fine."

"You're not fine," she counters, and I *barely* stop myself from rolling my eyes at her.

Nadia is a fierce woman. I don't need her to kick my ass over an eye roll.

"I'm *fine*," I repeat and narrow my eyes at her.

"What is it with the Martinelli brothers and being so fucking stubborn?" she asks as she turns back in her seat and scowls out the windshield.

"It's just part of our charm," Carmine says, but Nadia shakes her head.

"No, actually, it's not charming. It's dumb. He's going to hurt himself if he keeps overworking like that."

As if I have a choice. I can't exactly tell her that I sleep when the fucking *president* says I can.

So, I just grunt and watch Denver whiz by outside the window. The few hours it took to get here is, unfortunately, valuable time wasted. Time that I could have spent trying to find Ivie.

Jesus, where is she? What are they doing to her? And *who the fuck* are *they*?

"Almost there," Rocco mutters and sends me a sympathetic smile.

I know my brothers are aware of the massive crush I have on Ivie. I've never had a *crush* on anyone in my fucking life. But I saw her once, and that was all it took.

I know that Rocco and Carmine don't understand my attraction. That's because she's a little awkward and has a classic, girl-next-door look about her that I find absolutely hot as hell. She's not the type that would usually turn my head, and my siblings know it.

In the past, that may have been true.

But Ivie attracts me in every damn way. She's funny and sweet. *So* damn sweet. We've spent a little time on the phone, talking. I'm not much of a talker, but it comes so easily with Ivie.

How my brothers *don't* see the amazing woman she is, is beyond me.

I know that a relationship—hell, a *future*—with Ivie is out of the question for someone like me. My job consumes my life, and what's left over belongs to my family. Between the government and the mafia, I've killed more than any one man should. My time doesn't belong to me.

But if things were different, if I were free to be my own man, I would scoop Ivie up and make her mine in a heartbeat.

"She looks worse than the day she found out that Rich was a lying asshole," Nadia says as we pull into Annika's drive and see the woman standing in the doorway, waiting for us.

Her eyes are red-rimmed from crying, her nose chapped from wiping it too much. And when Nadia hurries to her and engulfs Annika in a hug, the other woman falls apart once more.

"Let's go inside," Carmine says, urging the women into the house and to the living room.

When Annika's seated and wiping her wet eyes, Carmine speaks again.

"Now, tell us again *exactly* what happened."

"Okay." Annika takes a long, deep breath and then tells us again about seeing the call from Ivie, but how she let it go to voicemail because she was getting into the shower and how she didn't remember about the call until this morning.

"So I finally listened to the message, and my blood ran cold."

"Play it," I say, sitting next to her as she pulls it up on her phone, taps the screen, and it starts to play.

"I'm sorry, I don't know a Laryssa. I'm Ivie. And we're

closed for the day. But if you'd like to make an appointment, I can help you with that."

"You know, I thought for a long time that your father was an imbecile. Stupid. He didn't cover his tracks well. But you're different. You covered your tracks very well. And I know that you couldn't have done that alone. Which tells me that your father isn't as stupid as I thought."

"I don't know what you could possibly want from me. I'm just living my life."

"And a nice life it is," the man says. "Good for you, Laryssa. I couldn't make your father pay for his sins when he was alive—and we both know that those sins were many. But now I've found you. Now, don't do something silly like try to get away. You're coming with me. And you're going to pay for the sins of your father."

There's a pause.

"There, now. Come along, Laryssa. We have plenty of work to do."

"After that, it's dead air for a couple of minutes, and then it ends," Annika says, locking her phone.

"Do you recognize his voice?" I ask her.

"No. I didn't recognize his face, either."

My head whips up. "You saw his face?"

"Yes, we have security cameras at the spa, of course. I looked at the footage, but I don't know who he is."

"I can find out," I reply. "I'll need to see it."

Annika nods, but Carmine shakes his head.

"He kept calling her Laryssa. That's not her name. Could she be a victim of mistaken identity?"

"No," Annika says softly and then stands to pace the room. "I can't believe I'm about to tell you this, but she's in danger, and you *have* to know."

My hands curl into fists.

"Know what?" I demand.

"Ivie's real name is Laryssa Pavlov. Her father was a Bulgarian asshole, but she escaped him when she was young. Made a new life for herself—one she could be proud of."

I can't believe what I'm hearing. After all the hours Ivie and I spent talking, she never told me any of this.

"So, this guy really is trying to punish her for her father's sins," Rocco says, blowing out a breath.

My brother's eyes haven't left Annika. It's no surprise he doesn't give me a hard time about Ivie. He, too, longs for someone he can't have.

It's a shitty situation to be in.

"What was her father's name?"

"Ivan. Ivan Pavlov," Annika says. "I can't tell you much about her past. She told me the story in confidence, but this definitely has something to do with her father."

"Get me that footage so I can find this motherfucker and get Ivie home where she belongs."

"Of course," Annika says, reaching for her laptop.

"I need to transfer this file to my system," I inform her, already tapping the keys on her computer. "I can find out who he is by running the face through some software and a database I have."

My hands fly over the keyboard, and then I reach into my bag for my laptop and get to work again, fingers flying.

When the screen simply says *Searching...* for what feels like a fucking year, I want to punch my hand through a wall.

But, finally, an image and bio appear on the screen.

"Boris Nicolov, fifty-eight. Bulgarian. Last known address is in New York. Looks like I'm going to the east coast."

I stand, and Rocco joins me. "Maybe you should do some more digging before you head off on a wild goose chase."

I push my brother against the wall and get up in his face.

"Get the fuck out of my way."

"Hey." His hands come up in surrender. "I'm not *in* your way. I'm just, you know, trying to be the voice of reason."

"Either you'll help me, or I'll do this without you."

"You know we'll help," Nadia says.

"I'll inform the Sergi family that we'll be on their turf for this," Carmine adds, referencing another mafia family. No one just shows up on another family's turf. You always let them know in advance.

"I didn't even think of that," I mutter and rub my hand down my face. "Thanks. Let's do this."

"Keep me posted," Annika says as she hurries

behind us to the door. "I guess I could have shown you all of this while you were still in Seattle."

"It's better in person," I reply and then reach back to squeeze her hand. "And this way, we're closer to New York than we were a few hours ago."

She offers me a watery smile, and Nadia, Carmine, and I all hurry back to the car.

Rocco hangs back to say something to Annika that has her tearing up again, then he jumps in the car with us, and we're off to the airfield.

"What did you say to her?" I ask quietly.

"It doesn't matter."

CHAPTER 2

~IVIE~

*M*y head is pounding. I can't see well because my eyes are blurry from the multiple slaps across the face that this asshole seems to enjoy handing out.

I don't know where I am. After he plunged the needle into my arm at the clinic, I blacked out. This room is dark, with no windows. And I'm sitting in a chair, my hands tied behind my back, just like the James Bond movies.

"You're going to tell me," he says. His voice has remained calm the entire time. How long has it been? It feels like weeks.

"I've told you over and over again, I *don't know.*"

"I don't believe you." His lips spread into a thin line. "My associates and I will be *very* disappointed if you don't tell me where he hid the money. And they'll be here soon."

"My father couldn't keep a dollar in his pocket," I reply. "He spent money, his or anyone else's, as soon as it landed in his hand. If he had your money, I'm sure he spent it long before he died and went to hell."

His eyes narrow. "You didn't like your father."

"Of course, I didn't. He was a pitiful excuse for a human being, and I ran away the first opportunity I got. And let me just say, at fifteen, it wasn't like I could hide easily. But he also never came looking, so there was no love lost, was there?"

I firm my lips and blink the tears from my eyes. Not from crying. No, this asshole isn't going to make me blubber like a baby. The water is from that last slap.

The man has a hell of a right arm.

He sighs and shakes his head.

"It's too much money for you not to know where it is," he insists. "So, we're going to have to get a little rougher."

He reaches over to a table and retrieves a pair of needle-nose pliers and bolt cutters.

"It would be a shame to start removing fingers from those dainty little hands."

"I. Don't. Know. Anything."

"I. Don't. Fucking. Believe. You."

He leans in and almost touches my nose with his. I can see light flecks of gold in his green eyes. And something starts to spread through me.

Not just anger. Not just fear and frustration.

Determination.

18

"I'm going to take off your fingers and then your toes. And if that still doesn't make you talk, I'm going to poke those pretty blue eyes out."

"There's one thing you didn't think of," I reply evenly. His eyes narrow just a bit, and I smile widely. "You forgot to tie my feet."

And with that, I pull my knees to my chest and kick out with all my might, plowing the soles of my feet right into this asshole's gut, sending him flying backward.

His arms flail, and he trips on a broken floorboard.

And then, as if in slow motion, he hits his head on the corner of a table and falls to the ground, blood gushing from his head.

His eyes are empty.

He's not breathing.

"Oh my God," I whisper, staring at him in horror. "Oh, shit. Shit shit shit. I *killed* him."

I look around at the plain walls and the single door behind me that must lead to the outside.

But I can't move. My hands are not tied to the chair, they're tethered to the floor, the rope through a metal ring. So it's not even like I can scooch my way over to the door and make noise.

I'm *stuck*.

I knew I was going to die in this room. Even if I'd told him what he wanted to know, even if I *could*, he would have killed me as soon as I did. I knew I wasn't leaving here alive.

But now I have to die by starvation and without water? I would have rather he put a bullet in my head.

I sigh and stare at the man. I don't know him. I have no idea what his name is, or how he knew my father. Obviously, my father double-crossed him on some deal. He mentioned his *colleagues*.

Who are they?

I don't even know how long my father's been dead. When this guy told me that he couldn't make my dad pay before he died, it was the first I'd heard of his demise.

I'm not surprised. He would have only been in his mid-to-late fifties, but he'd lived a hard, dangerous life.

For me, he died when I was fifteen, and I ran out of that horrible place in New York.

"I'm going to have to sit here and watch him decompose," I whisper in horror. "He's going to smell and get disgusting. Jesus, why do I have to be so clumsy? Leave it to me to send his head into the corner of a table just right."

I try to stand and attempt to work my way around so I can untie my hands, but I only succeed in almost dislocating my shoulder.

That won't help anything.

"Did he say his associates would be here soon? Oh, hell, I *am* going to die here. They're going to kill me."

I bite my lip. My heart starts to race. I haven't had a panic attack in a long time, but I'm on the verge now.

I'm stuck with a corpse, and bad men are on their way to kill me.

I'm a sitting duck.

"I didn't even get to tell Annika that I love her," I wail, feeling horribly sorry for myself. "Or have sex with Shane. Or even just spend time with him! I'm halfway to falling in love with him already, and now I'll never get to finish. I won't get to see the sun or eat raspberries in ice cream or go to the ocean."

Now, tears well up in my eyes. I thought I was safe. My cover was iron-clad. How did this asshole find me?

I hear rustling on the other side of the door and freeze.

This is it. This is how it ends.

But I won't go down without a fight, damn it.

I hear the door open, and then everything happens so fast. I lash out, kicking and yelling.

"I won't make this easy on you, motherfucker! You may kill me, but I'll kick your ass first."

"Hey, hey, hey." The voice is soothing, and when I open the eyes I didn't realize I'd closed, I see Shane standing in front of me, then kneeling to look me in the eyes. "It's us."

"Us?"

I glance around to see Shane's brothers and Nadia, one of my very best friends in the world.

Carmine squats next to *him*, checking for a pulse. "Dead."

"You killed him?" Nadia asks as Shane gently rubs

his fingers through my hair, and Rafe works on the ropes.

"Yeah. My clumsiness paid off." I tell them how it happened. "But we have to get out of here. He said he had associates on their way here. That's who I thought you were."

"In and out," Shane says, seeming to remind them all of their mission. "We deal with the rest later."

"What's the rest?"

"Plane's ready," Rafe says with a nod. Suddenly, my hands are free, and Shane lifts me into his arms.

"We're getting you out of here, little dove."

I lay my head on his shoulder, suddenly so tired I can't keep my eyes open. I feel weird. Dizzy.

And then I feel nothing at all.

"WAKE UP, SWEET GIRL," Shane croons in my ear. I feel like I must be in heaven. Surely, I've died, and heaven is a place where Shane's voice wraps around me and makes me feel safe. "Come on, Ivie, I need you to open those gorgeous eyes for me."

My eyes flutter open, and I see Shane leaning over me, smiling down at me softly.

"There you are," he says. "You scared me for a minute there."

"I'm in a bed." I frown and glance around. "Are we *flying*?"

"Yes, we're flying back to Denver."

"Wait." I sit up and press my hand to my head. "Weren't we already in Denver?"

Shane sits next to me, takes my hand, and then kisses my fingers, making my stomach jump.

"What do you remember?"

"I remember being taken out of the clinic. I was drugged. Then I woke up in a shitty room and got beat up a bit. Ended up killing my captor *on accident*, and then you arrived."

"I suppose that's the CliffsNotes version," he murmurs. "Honey, he took you to New York. We found you in a basement in Queens."

I blink, completely baffled. "I was passed out that long? I wonder what he drugged me with?"

"As do I," Shane says, examining me. "Does anything hurt?"

"I'm a little stiff and sore from having my hands tied behind me for so long, but other than that, I'll live."

"When I saw his handprint on your cheek, I wanted to kill him myself," he admits. His voice is mild, but by the look in his eyes, I can see that he means every word.

"I kicked him," I say, thinking it over. "He was up in my face, trying to intimidate me, and I just brought my feet up and kicked him in the gut, hard. He jerked back, tripped, and then fell against the table."

"That was too good of a death for him."

I blow out a sigh. "Yeah, well, it was fast. I don't know who the hell he was."

"I do," Shane says. "We'll talk about it all when we get to my place."

"*Your* place?"

He just looks at me with those gorgeous brown eyes that always seem to hypnotize me.

"Shane, I have to work. Annika needs me. Oh my God, Annika!"

"We've already told her that we found you safe and sound," he assures me. "We'll stop and see her before we go to my place in the mountains."

"Shane, I can't go with you to the mountains."

"And I can't let you go home," he says. "Not until we have a full picture of what's going on here. I'm going to keep you safe, no matter what. A little time away from work won't hurt anyone."

"I don't—"

"I'm not asking," he says, his voice sharp, and I gape up at him.

"I was just kidnapped once. I won't do it again, Shane. I care about you, and I enjoy being with you, but I'll live my life under *my* terms."

He rubs his hand over his lips in agitation. "I'm just trying to keep you safe."

My head is throbbing. "I don't want to have our first fight on this plane."

His expression softens, and then he chuckles. "Fair enough. Have you eaten?"

"My captor didn't offer me room service."

"Let's go eat something," he suggests and reaches out for my hand. He leads me into a different part of the plane where the others are seated. Carmine and Nadia are curled up on a loveseat, looking at an iPad. Rafe is staring out the window. All their heads come up when they hear us enter.

"How are you feeling, sugar?" Nadia asks, rushing over to hug me.

"I'll be okay. I'm hungry."

"I have a tray ready for you, miss." I look up at the formal voice and blink at the older gentleman who's smiling kindly at me. "I'm Charles, and I'm happy to help you today."

"Thank you." I glance up at Shane, but he just nods and gestures for me to sit at a table. Within a few seconds, Charles sets a charcuterie board full of cheeses, meats, nuts, and olives in front of me, and I immediately dig in. "This is awesome."

"What would you like to drink, miss?" the attendant asks.

"Water, please."

He nods and turns to fetch my drink. Shane sits opposite me, watching me wolf down the food.

"Want a cashew?" I ask him, holding out the nut.

"No, you eat," he says.

"How long has it been?" I ask, suddenly not sure how long the jerk had me. "Since I left the clinic?"

"About twenty-four hours," Rafe says.

"This is pathetic," I reply with a laugh. "I just ate twenty-four hours ago and I'm starving. I can't even consider this a fast."

"Killing people burns a lot of calories," Nadia says.

"And so does adrenaline," Carmine adds.

"True. And probably the drugs. What a crazy turn of events. So much for living a boring life."

"I have questions." I look up at Shane's statement, and my stomach tenses. "Questions I need answers to so I can do my job here and protect you."

"I'm not your job."

His jaw clenches. "Yes. You are."

"No. I'm not." I eat a grape and consider him. "Don't get me wrong. You'll never know how much I appreciate all of you for saving me. I shudder to think what might have happened to me if you hadn't come to find me. I would have died. Whether that was a long, slow death with a corpse decaying next to me, or a quick one when the other bad guys got there, I don't know. But I wouldn't have lived through it. So, I owe you a huge debt of gratitude that I can never repay."

"You don't *owe* us anything," Nadia says. "This is what family does."

"We rescue each other from kidnappers?" I ask, suddenly feeling emotional. Annika and Nadia are the only family I've ever really had.

"Among other things," Nadia says with a wink.

"I'll answer your questions," I say with a sigh. "But

can I please eat this delicious cheese and get some rest first?"

"I don't see why not," Shane replies, seemingly placated for now. I need to think about how much I'm going to tell him.

It's not that I don't trust him. It's that I'm embarrassed. Of what and who I come from. Of what I had to do as a child. And I've always hoped that my past was so far in the rearview that it was forgotten.

Over.

But now, out of the blue, it's front and center. Exactly where I never wanted it to be.

But, worst of all, I'm afraid that when I tell Shane the whole truth, his feelings for me, whatever they may be, will change. He'll lose that spark of interest in his eyes whenever he sees me. He'll want nothing to do with me.

And that will hurt most of all. Because even though we don't know each other all that well yet, he's come to mean a lot to me.

"Looks like we're landing," Rafe says as the plane starts its descent. "We'll be at Annika's in about an hour or so."

CHAPTER 3

~SHANE~

"*Y*ou really should go with him," Annika insists for the third time, but Ivie just shakes her head stubbornly.

"I'm needed *here*," she says. "I have a job and a life to see to. I can't let them win."

"Staying *safe*," I insist through gritted teeth, "isn't letting anyone win. It's being smart."

"I'm not trying to be difficult," Ivie says with a long sigh. "Honestly, I'm not. But I almost lost this life, and I love it. I've worked hard for it. And, damn it, I want to get back to living it."

"Nothing says that you won't be back at it in just a few days," Carmine points out. "In the meantime, hang out with Shane until all of this can get resolved."

Ivie firms her lips, and I decide that I'd like to tie her up and carry her to my place myself.

But I don't think she'd like that either.

28

"Fine. If you won't go, I'll stay." I stand and shove my hand through my hair. "I'll stay with you."

"Shane—"

"Did you really think that after what happened to you over the past twenty-four hours that I'd just walk away?" The outburst is unusual for me, but I can't hold it in any longer. "Because the answer to that is fuck no. You come with me, or I stay with you. That's the way it's going to be. You choose."

Her little chin comes up, and she meets my eyes. "Fine. I have a spare bedroom."

"Fine."

"I think you're both tired," Nadia says and pats Ivie on the shoulder. "Go get some rest. Fight in the morning."

"Good idea," Annika agrees. "I'm so, *so* relieved that you're home. And I'm sorry that I let you down."

"Stop apologizing," Ivie insists. "You didn't know. I'm just glad you listened to the message and sent the cavalry in to save me."

"Oh, this is Uncle Igor," Annika says as her phone rings. "He's been worried sick. Hello, Uncle. Yes, she's here. She's safe. The Martinellis are with her. I'll let her know."

"Your family is the best," Ivie whispers.

"They love you," Nadia says with a shrug. "Was Papa angry?"

"Livid," Annika confirms. "And very concerned. We all have been. We're just relieved that she's safe."

Tired hugs are exchanged. Once outside, I pull Rocco and Carmine aside.

"I would rather be at my place. I can protect her better there."

"I know," Carmine says. "We're going to stick close for a few days, just in case."

"I'll be around, as well," Rocco says and gestures to the two additional vehicles on the street. "I had these delivered. Figured we'd go our separate ways."

"Appreciate it," I reply with a nod. "I'll let you know if anything comes up."

"Same here," Carmine says, and the three of us go to our separate vehicles to drive away.

"How did these cars get here?" Ivie asks after she buckles up.

"Rocco had them delivered."

She frowns at me as I back out of the driveway. "How?"

"We have people, Ivie. In every major city of this country, and several around the world. All we have to do is make a phone call, and certain things happen."

She chews her lip and then frowns when she realizes that I'm headed right for her house.

"How do you know where I live?"

"I dropped you off there one night, remember?"

"I'm surprised *you* remember."

I have an excellent memory when it comes to things I want.

"Are you mad at me for not going with you?" she asks.

"Yes." The answer is short and simple. "I'm frustrated because it would be easier to keep you safe at my home. I feel blind this way. But I'm not going to force you to do anything you don't want to do, so we'll try it your way."

She blows out a raspberry through her lips and then lets out a gasp of surprise when I turn into her driveway.

"My door is open," she says. "I know I didn't leave it like that when I left for work yesterday."

"Stay here. Lock the doors."

I jump out of the car and immediately pull my sidearm from its holster. Before rushing inside, I make a quick loop around the house to see if I can detect any movement.

From out here, it looks empty.

When I make my way back to the front door, I ease it open farther and step inside, raising my weapon when a figure walks across the living room and snaps on the light.

"For fuck's sake, Ivie, I told you to wait outside."

But she's not listening to me. Her eyes are trained on the destruction in her home. The place has been ransacked, turned over and destroyed.

"Oh my God," she breathes.

"Stay with me," I order her, my voice sharp. "Do you hear me? Ivie."

"I hear you." She slips her hand into mine, and I lead her through the house, to each room, with my weapon drawn in case anyone is still here.

"We're alone," I say at last when we're standing in her bedroom.

She slips her hand from mine and hurries over to her closet. I follow her over and see her stumble over clothes, then peel back the carpet in a corner, open a hidden spot on the floor, and pull out a small box.

"They didn't take it," she breathes in relief. "My mother's wedding ring. It's the only thing I have from her, and I could never replace it."

She hugs the box to her chest and allows her gaze to roam over the mess.

"I guess you're getting your way," she says at last.

"It's not a competition." I take her hand and pull her to her feet. "Honey, I just want you to be as safe as possible."

"Well, it doesn't look like that'll be here. I'll try to pull some things together and be ready in a few minutes."

I nod and step out of the room so I can text my brothers, letting them know about the change of plans. I also call my father to keep him posted. We've been feeding him information since all of this began.

When these assholes took Ivie, they pissed off two powerful mafia families in the process.

They're fucked.

"I'm ready." Ivie has a small suitcase that's seen

better days, a tote filled to the brim, and a purse, which she retrieved from Annika earlier. "The bastards ruined my Louis Vuitton handbag. It was a gift."

"It can be replaced."

"Do you know how much those things cost?" she demands. "Anyway. It's just a purse. But it pissed me off. I'm taking the few valuable things I have with me, some clothes and toiletries, and that's about it."

"That's all you'll need," I assure her. I can feel the sadness and despair radiating off her as we walk through her little house to the front door. She locks it as I put her bags in the car, and then we're off again. "We have a bit of a drive ahead of us."

She just nods and stares out the window. So, I decide to let her be. A lot has happened. She's exhausted.

My questions can be answered tomorrow.

"So, you live way out here in the middle of nowhere," she says when I turn onto my dirt road.

I let my caretaker know that I was on my way, and the make and model of the car we're in, so the gate automatically swings open at our arrival.

I imagine Curt is sitting in his little cabin, watching the monitor.

"Yes. I do."

It's dark now. I think this has been the longest

damn day of my life. We're quiet, as we were the entire drive, as I navigate the Lexus past the helicopter landing pad, my shooting range, a barn, and an underground bunker—all of which is out of view in the darkness.

I pull up to my house and cut the engine. Several lights are on, also thanks to Curt.

"Is someone else here?" she asks, then turns to me with wide eyes. "Oh my God, do you have a girlfriend?"

"No. No girlfriend."

"Why are the lights on?"

"I have a friend who lives in a cabin here on the property," I begin as I open my door, then hurry around to open hers. I take her hand and help her out of the car. "He's an old Army buddy. He likes to be alone, and he's damn good at his job. So it works well for both of us. You might meet him."

She nods and follows me up the stairs to my back door. I set her bags down and open the door, then gesture her inside.

This entrance leads right into my kitchen. "When I built this house, I wanted it to look like an old farmhouse. To blend in and look rustic at the base of the mountain."

"I love it," she breathes, looking around with tired, sapphire eyes. "It's modern and beautiful, but also has that old-fashioned vibe to it."

"Bingo. Come on, it's not a huge place. I'll show you around. This is the living area. TV and all that jazz.

There's a sunroom over there, but I've never gotten around to furnishing it."

I swing into the guest room and set her bags on the floor, switching on the light. "This is your room. Make yourself at home. There's a bathroom through that door. Walk-in closet here. When the sun's up, you'll have a great view of the mountains."

"Thank you." She runs her fingertips over the comforter on the queen-sized bed. "Where will you be?"

"Down here," I reply and take her hand, leading her just down the hall to my bedroom. "This is my room. Nothing too fancy, but it's home."

She takes in my king-sized bed and the chair in the corner.

"I have another bathroom through there. If you go up the stairs by the front door, there's a loft and another guest room. If you'd rather have that one—"

"No, the one you've given me is great." She offers me a forced smile. "It'll be perfect."

Seeing her like this, distant and sad, tears at my heart, so I pull her to me and wrap my arms around her. I bury my lips in her hair and kiss her gently.

"Besides the obvious, tell me why you're miserable."

"Because you don't want me here, and I feel like I'm crashing into your life, and—"

"Whoa." I pull back and stare down at her. "I'm the one who *told* you that you'd be better off coming here with me."

"Only because you're feeling overprotective," she insists. "I'm just a burden, and I hate that."

"Let's get something straight." I tip up her chin, making her look me in the eyes. "I don't do much that I don't want to in this life. If I didn't want to be with you, I'd have put you in a safe house and staffed it with security. I want you here, Ivie. Hell, we're friends. We've spent time together. And God knows I think you're the sexiest damn thing I've ever seen in my life."

She lets out a snort, and I narrow my eyes.

"Is something I said funny?"

"You don't have to lay it on so thick."

I don't reply. I simply step into her and lay my lips on hers. Gently. As far as first kisses go, it's not the way I'd planned to do it, but it works. She tastes like sin, and the little noise she makes in the back of her throat as she melts against me would make a weaker man lose control.

But I end the kiss and smile down at her.

"Does that feel like you're a burden?"

She shakes her head.

"You're here because I care about you, I want you safe, and I'm the only one I trust to do that correctly. I get the bonus of having you with me pretty much nonstop for the foreseeable future."

"Thank you," she whispers.

"Are you hungry?"

"Yes, actually."

"Good. Me, too. I'll fix us something."

I lead her back out to the kitchen and get her settled on a stool while I set about making us a couple of omelets. Nothing fancy but full of veggies and nutrients to get us through until morning.

"So, was it your caretaker who stocked your kitchen for you?"

"Yeah. Curt keeps this place running when I'm gone. I haven't been here in..." I stop, lean on the counter and think about it. "Fuck, I haven't been home in two weeks."

"Where were you?"

There's no way I'll ever tell Ivie about the horrors I see when I'm out on a mission. So I just smile at her and shrug a shoulder. "Here and there."

"I have questions," she murmurs.

"That makes two of us."

She swallows hard and then nods. "We'll talk tomorrow, okay?"

"That works for me. I haven't slept in at least three days, and you look like you're ready to drop."

"I don't remember ever being this tired before," she admits.

"Are you finished there?" I gesture to her half-eaten plate.

"Yeah, I'm done."

I clear our dishes and then kiss Ivie's forehead. "Let's go to bed, then."

I escort her to her door, and after she closes it, I pad to another room that I didn't show her. This isn't as big as the operation I have in the basement, but it's a convenient space where I have monitors set up to show me the security cameras around the property.

With roughly a thousand acres, there's a lot of ground to cover. I shuffle through the live feeds, satisfied that everything looks calm tonight. After I send a note of thanks to Curt, I shut down everything and head to bed.

But at least an hour later, after a shower and some reading, I can't get comfortable. It's not like me to toss and turn like this after an exhausting operation like the one I just finished. Add to it the adrenaline of looking for Ivie, and my body is just about ready to quit on me.

But I can't get comfortable. I wonder how she's doing down the hall. Was she able to settle in and get comfortable? Is she having nightmares after her ordeal?

Does she need anything?

I'm just about to get up and go check on her when there's a light knock on my door.

"Come in."

The door slowly opens, and there's Ivie, standing in the moonlight.

"Can I sleep in that chair?" she asks, pointing to the chair in the corner of the room.

"No." I shift to the side and peel back the covers. "You can come sleep here."

"Really?"

"Come on, honey."

She closes the door behind her and turns to walk my way. Suddenly, she trips and lands on the bed, hard.

"Sorry, I didn't see the floor there."

I chuckle and tuck her in next to me, spoon up behind her, and breathe her in. She, too, had a shower, and her hair smells amazing.

But I don't want to ravage her. I want to *hold* her. Another new emotion for me.

"You're naked," she says, glancing over her shoulder at me.

"Yes, ma'am. Do you want me to put something on?" I kiss her hair, still breathing her in.

"No, it's okay. Just another surprise, that's all. I was scared," she admits with a whisper.

"No need to be," I whisper back. "I'm right here. I've got you. Just sleep, baby."

CHAPTER 4

~IVIE~

I hurt. My neck is sore, my ribs ache, and I feel like I got hit by a bus.

And then the events of the past few days come into my mind, and I sigh, even before opening my eyes.

No wonder I ache.

But then last night comes into focus, and I can't help but smile. I was so scared in that bedroom by myself. I'm in a strange place, in the middle of the woods, and people are trying to kill me.

At least, I think they are.

I didn't want to be alone. And Shane didn't turn me away. Instead, he welcomed me into his bed, wrapped his big, strong arms around me, and held me all night. Naked.

So, so naked.

When I woke up in the middle of the night with a

jolt from a nightmare, he soothed me until we both fell back to sleep.

I can't remember the last time I felt this protected.

Have I ever been?

I shift a bit and realize that Shane's hand landed on my left breast in his slumber.

I glance down, and sure enough... His huge hand rests over my breast, and I look up in surprise.

Damn, he has big hands. I'm a well-endowed girl in the boob department, but his hand completely covers me.

I blink rapidly. I wonder if that means he's *big* in other areas.

I can't hold the snort in, but then try to cover it up with a fake sneeze.

"Go back to sleep." Shane's voice is deep and gravelly, and he shifts, dragging his hand down my breast to my ribs as if we do this every morning.

"I'm asleep."

"Then why are you talking to me?"

I grin and turn to glance at him but end up hitting him in the chin with the ball of my shoulder.

"Ouch."

"Sorry." I wiggle around until I'm facing him but cover my mouth with the blanket—because, morning breath. "So sorry."

"You don't sound sorry."

I just smile from behind the blanket. Shane opens an eye and then chuckles. "How are you this morning?"

"Oh, I hurt everywhere."

"Wait. What?" He sits up, pulling the blanket from my mouth. It pools at his waist.

Jesus, his chest and abs are sculpted.

"Wow," I whisper, wanting to reach out and touch him.

"What do you mean you hurt everywhere?"

"Calm down." I slowly sit up beside him and wince with the effort. "He kicked me in the ribs a couple of times so they're a bit sore today. And I have a headache. Probably from being slapped."

"I want to fucking kill him." The words are said with perfect calm, just as matter-of-factly as if he were giving me a weather report.

"I got to do that," I reply. "It was an accident, but I can't say that I'm sorry. Does that make me a bad person?"

"No." He shuffles to the opposite side of the bed, and I see a glimpse of his tight, bare ass before he slips on his jeans and turns to me with them still unfastened. His dark hair is rumpled from sleep. His eyes not quite awake. And seeing him like this does things to me.

Sexy things.

I clear my throat and look away.

"I have to unpack," I say and stand to escape the room.

"Wait."

I turn back to him and see he's gazing at me with a lazy grin. "I'm going to eventually tumble you into this bed and have my way with you, Ivie. But not while you're hurting, and not until I've had time to kiss the hell out of you first."

What in the hell am I supposed to say to that?

I start to speak, but it just comes out as a squeak, so I clear my throat and just say, "Okay."

"You unpack. I'll make breakfast. Do you like French toast?"

So much for going gluten-free. "I love it."

"Excellent." He pulls a black T-shirt over his head, covering up all that glorious, tanned skin and those abs, so I turn to go unpack. "Ivie?"

"Yeah?" I turn back to see his hot, dark eyes roaming up and down my body.

"Nice night thing."

I glance down at my simple red sleep shirt. It says *Knocked Out* on the front. There's nothing particularly sexy or interesting about it.

"Huh?"

He just grins, and his eyes fall level with my butt. I realize that it barely covers my round ass.

He's been staring at my black panties and bare cheeks.

So, with a sassy turn, I let him enjoy the show.

Shane's laughter follows me down the hall to the room that he offered me last night. I like Shane's home. It's simple. The kitchen is glorious, and I would love to work some magic in there. I love the farmhouse vibe.

Joanna Gaines would be proud.

But it's evident that a bachelor lives here. There are no little touches like pretty towels, decorative rugs, or pieces of artwork hung here and there.

As wonderful as this place is now, it could be truly beautiful.

But it's clean, it's safe, and for now, that's all I really need.

I start by unpacking my tote bag. I have all of my bathroom supplies in here, so I just take it with me to the restroom and unpack my razor, special hair mask, and other shower needs. I used my shampoo and conditioner last night but didn't bother to unpack the rest.

I set up the sink with my favorite soap, toothbrush, and toothpaste, and all of my skin-care bottles—which is more than most people use, but I work at a medi-spa. Having flawless skin is important and healthy.

I toss the empty tote into the closet and move onto the suitcase.

I've had this thing for as long as I can remember. It's the same one I had when I fled my father's house all those years ago. I've added other luggage here and there over the years, but this one belonged to my mother, so I'll likely keep it until it's nothing but rags.

I tuck my jeans into an empty drawer in the dresser and hang my shirts in the closet, then stow my undies and bras in another drawer. I only brought a couple of pairs of shoes and lay them in the bottom of the closet.

When the suitcase is empty, I zip it shut, pick it up to stow it away, and hear a rattle.

"Did a button fall off of something? That would be my luck," I mutter as I unzip it and glance inside.

But I don't see anything.

I pick it up and shake it.

Still rattling.

The lining of the bag has several tears.

"Something must have slipped through." I unzip the liner and reach my hand in, feeling around. When I come up with a small, black flash drive, I scowl.

"Oh."

"I'm telling you, I don't want to."

"I do not care what you want, Laryssa." Father just flicks his wrist as if he's batting at an annoying fly. "You'll do as I say without question."

I want to stomp my feet. I want to yell at him and tear my hair out in frustration. Why won't he listen to me? Why is he so awful?

I'm so sick and tired of being his errand girl. Of going into scary places with mean people and men who like to cop a feel as I walk past them, just to drop off these stupid things.

How important can this be, anyway?

I turn and stomp away, pissed and hurt that my father can't show me even an ounce of kindness.

Rather than take this where he wants me to, I reach into my tiny closet for Mommy's suitcase and tuck it away inside. I don't want to go to that place again.

It smells, and the men look at me in weird ways that make me feel dirty.

I'm not going.

Father won't know. It's not like he'll ever find out that I didn't take it.

I secure it back in the closet and then slip my feet into my shoes, making a hasty escape out of the dirty little house we live in. I'll go down to the diner where they're nice to me and let me eat all of the ice cream I want.

I shake my head and stare down at the flash drive in my hand.

"Shane!" I run out of the bedroom to the kitchen, where Shane's just plating up our breakfast.

"You're just in time." He smiles as he glances up, but when he sees my face, the smile fades. "What's wrong?"

"This." I hold it up and stare at him in horror. "I think this could be something."

"What kind of something, Ivie?"

I swallow hard and wish with all my might that we didn't have to have the conversation about to come.

"I guess it's time to talk," I say.

"Okay. Am I about to lose my appetite?"

"Maybe. I don't know." I set the flash drive on the counter, unable to hold it anymore. "My birth name is Laryssa Pavlov. My father worked with some kind of government intelligence agency in Bulgaria, and when I was very small, we moved to the US. I don't remember being in Bulgaria. My mother died when I was four. My father raised me, so to speak."

I sit and stare at the French toast and then decide…*fuck it.* I'm hungry. I'm going to eat. So, I start slathering it in butter and syrup and keep talking.

"I don't honestly know what he was into. I was his minion. Not his daughter." I take a bite of bread and sigh in happiness. "He made me run errands for him in New York. I had to deliver things, usually like *that*"—I point at the flash drive with my fork—"to men who were creepy and handsy."

"Handsy?"

I look up at him. "They liked to look, and they liked to grope. And my father didn't give a shit. Anyway, I was fifteen, and I hated him with every fiber of my being. I hated having to do his bidding. I didn't know what he was into, but I knew it was illegal, and if I got caught, I could get into trouble. So, I told him, flat-out, that I wasn't going to do it anymore."

"And how did that go over?"

"Not well." I shrug and take another bite. "He hit me. Threatened to pimp me out to the creepy dudes who liked to look. And then these guys came banging on the door and started to beat *him* up pretty bad.

"I'd already packed my bag, ready to run as soon as I had the chance. And what better opportunity than when he was getting the shit kicked out of him? So, I grabbed my suitcase, the one currently in your closet, and I ran. I never saw him again."

His eyes narrow on me as he, too, eats his breakfast. "Where did you get that?" He points at the flash drive.

"I'd forgotten that I'd hidden it a couple of weeks before I ran away. He wanted me to deliver it to one of those places, and I was just so *sick* of it, Shane. It was awful. So, instead, I hid it away in my mom's suitcase. I hid it in the interior lining, you know?"

He nods, and I keep going.

"I forgot about it. For all these years. Just now, after I finished unpacking, I heard the rattle and found it."

"What's on it?"

"Your guess is as good as mine."

With our plates empty, Shane retrieves the drive and takes my hand.

"Let's go."

He keys in a code on a locked door and leads me down a long stairway. When we reach the basement, he turns on the light, and all I can do is stare.

Monitors fill one wall. There are computers, printers, maps, papers...all spread out around the room. It looks like a command center, and as I stare at Shane now, as he punches at a keyboard, and some of the monitors come to life, I realize that's exactly what it is.

A command center.

"Are you James Bond?"

His fingers stop tapping, and he turns to me with a slow smile. "I'm better than him, honey. Come here."

I join him at the desk, leaning over his shoulder as he slips the flash drive into a slot and what looks like gibberish fills a screen.

"What is that?" I wonder aloud as I stare at it. "It looks like some kind of weird hieroglyphics."

"Whatever's on here is encrypted."

He's still typing, but even I can see that he's going about it the wrong way.

"You're doing it wrong."

His sexy dark brow quirks above his eye. "Excuse me?"

"May I?"

"By all means." He scoots the chair back and tugs me into his lap, and for half a second, I'm not sure what I'm supposed to be doing. Shane's nose nuzzles my ear.

"Well?"

"Well, what?"

He chuckles. "You asked for the control, Ivie."

I love that he calls me Ivie. That everything I told him in the kitchen doesn't seem to bother him in the least.

I get to work, tapping keys, trying to break the failsafe on this thing.

"I was something of a hacker in college," I mutter as I meet a wall, curse, and then keep going. "I was already using Ivie as my name, but I had to make it legal without people asking a bunch of questions or requesting birth certificates."

"So you learned to *hack?*"

"I'm a bit of a nerd." I shrug and try to ignore his fingers doing delicious things to my back. "There. It's searching for it now."

I lean back into him as the computer does its thing and turn my face up to his.

"You're the sexiest nerd I've ever seen in my life."

I grin. "I'm not sexy or beautiful. I know it, and it's okay. I'm passable at best when I'm all gussied up."

"Who told you that?"

"No one needed to." *My father hammered home every damn day that I was a disappointment in the looks department.* "I can see myself in the mirror."

"Then you're looking at the wrong damn thing." He kisses my jawline while his hands roam over my ribs. "From the minute I saw you at Annika's wedding, I couldn't take my eyes off you. You're addictive, Ivie."

I want to snort. I want to laugh. This is a joke, right? Because no one's ever called me *addictive*. Pretty? Sure. You look nice? Occasionally. But never this.

However, based on the way he's touching me, I'd say he's not joking.

He cups my face and turns me to him. His lips are gentle on mine as they linger, tasting me, teasing the corner of my mouth until my nipples stand at attention.

He takes the kiss deeper, my fingers diving into his hair, and we're consumed by each other when the beeping starts.

"It's done," I whisper against his lips.

"Damn it," he replies, making me laugh.

When I turn back to the screen, I scowl. "This is just more gibberish."

"It's a language," Shane says.

"Oh, good. We can just plug it into Google Translate and call it a day." Shane stares at me as if I just suggested we jump into shark-infested waters. "What?"

"We absolutely can *not* use Google for this. Whoever's looking for this would be here in an hour. Now it's your turn to sit back and let me work my magic."

"Have at it."

I watch as he taps the keys, copies and pastes, then hits enter and waits.

"Did that just happen?"

"Fuck."

CHAPTER 5

"*D*id that just erase itself?" Ivie demands, panic laced through her sexy voice.

"It seems so."

"Damn it." She reaches out to start working on the keyboard again, but I stop her. "Maybe I can get it back."

"If we keep trying, it'll corrupt itself, and we won't get anything at all."

"Then what are we supposed to do?"

"I'm calling a friend." I pull my phone out of my pocket, tap the screen, and then reach out and push my fingers through Ivie's hair as I wait for him to answer.

"Cox."

"I need your help." I give him a brief report on what we have going on. "The sooner, the better."

"Yeah, I can look at it. Just send it through. I'll get to it later today."

"No, I need you to come here. I'm not sending this out anywhere."

There's a brief pause. "Are you in Colorado?"

"At the ranch," I confirm and wink at a waiting Ivie. "The sooner you can get here, the better. Wait, are you out of the country?"

"No, I'm in Seattle. I can be there later this afternoon."

"I owe you one."

"You owe me about a dozen."

He clicks off, and I methodically shut down the system and pull the drive out of the slot.

"So, who is Cox?" Ivie asks.

"Cameron Cox is a friend. An old Army buddy and the best computer genius in the country—maybe in the world. I've been on missions with him all over the globe. I'd trust him with my life, or yours."

"And he's based in Seattle?"

"On an island not far from the city," I confirm. "His family is there. He'll be here later today."

"And he's just going to drop everything and come here? Just like that?"

I lean back in the chair and watch her. I do enjoy looking at her. The way her hair falls around her face. I want to kiss the little beauty mark next to her eye.

"Cox and I have been through hell and back together. If you get a call asking for help, you help."

She nods, thinking it over. "If Annika or Nadia needed me, I'd be there in a heartbeat."

"Exactly."

"So, you were in the Army?" She follows me up the stairs, and I lock the door behind us. I've never had anyone break into my place, but if they did, that room is the last place I'd want an intruder.

"For a few years."

"But you still work for the government?"

I like Ivie. My feelings for her are strong, more intense than I've ever had for a woman before. And I trust her. That's not the issue. But most of what I do can't be talked about with anyone. Even if we were married, I couldn't tell her.

"I do work for the government here and there." We walk into the kitchen, and I set our dishes in the dishwasher.

"What kind of work?"

I sigh and lean on my hands. "I don't want to lie to you or mislead you. If you were anyone else, I'd say none of your damn business and go about my day, but you're not anyone else. I can't tell you what I do. Everything I do is classified. Locked up so tightly, only the president herself knows all the details."

Ivie's eyes widen in surprise. "So, you're a mobster *and* a government operative?" She swallows hard and sits on a stool.

"Okay, talk to me."

"You're exactly the type of man I've avoided all my life. All I ever wanted was a nice, simple life. Nothing illegal going on, nothing to be afraid of. And I had that

—until yesterday. I always saw myself with someone boring like an accountant or a small-business owner. Or just something *safe.*"

"You can still have those things." The words are out of my mouth before I can stop them. Ivie's mouth closes, and her brow furrows.

Jesus, I'm a grade-A asshole.

"Of course." She offers me a polite, fake smile. "I'll just be in my room."

"Ivie."

"I'm fine." That smile disappears as she turns to leave.

"Stop, damn it."

But she doesn't. She flees into the guest room and shuts the door, but I open it and walk right in after her.

"Ivie."

"I'm not upset," she says, but tears swim in her eyes, breaking my heart in two. "Really. You haven't made me any promises. I was silly to think that just because we talked a lot, and you flirted with me, and are so hell-bent on protecting me that this could go anywhere."

"You're not silly." I shove my hands into my pockets because I don't know what else to do with them. "You're not silly at all. I'm an asshole for chasing after you when I knew good and well that I could never have you."

She scowls at me now, and I don't even flinch because I deserve it.

"I'm right here," she says, spreading her arms wide. "I'm not married. And I'm not saying no. So why can't you have me?"

"Didn't you hear me out there? I can *never* tell you about my job, Ivie. Ever. I'll be out there in the world doing some really shady shit that you can never know about. And you said yourself that you don't want that kind of life. You want a stable one. And while I could always provide for you financially—"

"I don't want your money."

"—I can't promise you that I'll always come home from every mission alive."

She swallows hard. "So, what, you've just been playing with me for these months? Was I just something fun to do when you're not off doing God knows what, God knows where?"

"No." I push my hands through my hair, pissed at myself. "I told you earlier, you're addictive. I *hate* not being able to speak to you when I'm gone. And hearing your voice or seeing you is what I look forward to the most when I come back."

She shakes her head and crosses her arms over her chest. "I don't believe you. Shane, *I'm* not the girl who guys fall for like that. I'm the one they play with. Ask out on a dare. Laugh at me because I'm good with computers and am a little clumsy. I'm not Nadia or Annika."

"Stop it with this." Unable to hold myself back, I cross to her and take her shoulders in my hands, mindful that she's still sore from yesterday. "If that happened to you, it's because boys are fucked-up in the head. It had nothing to do with *you.*"

"Look." She shrugs out of my hold. "You don't owe me anything. It was only some harmless flirting. I get it. I'm a big girl, and you've just made it perfectly clear where we stand. Understood."

"Fuck." I drag my hands down my face in frustration. I *want* her. I want every inch of her, for today and for the rest of my fucking life. And that makes me the biggest, most selfish jerk in the world because this can't work. "Ivie, you're a beautiful woman. You're funny and smart, and your clumsiness makes you all the more fun. I think you're amazing."

"But you don't want me." She nods and motions for me to leave. "You can go."

"No, damn it." I advance on her and pull her against me, fold my lips over hers and take her. This kiss is desperate, full of fire and frustration. After a long moment, her hands fist in my shirt at my sides, and she holds on as I take us both on a ride. "I want you. I want you so badly it's fucking killing me."

"I'm *right here.*" A soft sob escapes her throat as I kiss my way down to her collarbone. "Wait."

She takes my face in her hands and looks deeply into my eyes.

"You're afraid."

I start to deny it, but she holds me tighter.

"You are. Why are you scared?"

I tip my forehead to hers and let out a long, even breath.

I'm afraid of falling in love with you and then leaving you here alone.

But I can't say that. I just can't. Not right now.

"I'm afraid of a lot of things," I say at last and brush my fingertips down her cheek. "You being hurt is at the top of the list."

Her eyes clear, and all of the anger and confusion from a moment ago just evaporates. What's left nearly takes my breath away.

"Don't fall in love with me, little dove."

"No. That would be ridiculous." Her lips twitch into a small smile. "Are we done fighting now?"

"I feel like that's a trick question."

"Looks like we are. Let's get out of this house. Show me around. I just have to change my clothes. Can we walk the ranch, or will we be in the car?"

I know what she's doing, and it won't work. But I don't want to see the happiness in her eyes disappear.

"We can walk it."

"Well, it's a good thing I brought some sneakers. I'll be ready in ten."

"Why do you have a bunker?"

We're standing at the opening, staring down into the black hole.

"Are you a prepper?" she asks before I can reply to the first question.

"I'm the king of preppers," I say with a laugh. "I'm always prepared for anything."

"I see that." She glances around. "Like the nuclear apocalypse."

"Hey, you never know, right?"

She narrows her eyes at me. "If there's a nuclear apocalypse, I don't want to survive it. Do you know how horrible it would be? *Horrible.* That's a solid 'no, thanks' for me."

I laugh and tuck her hair behind her ear. "This isn't here for that. If someone ever breached my property, and all hell broke loose, this is the most secure place on the ranch."

Her eyes go wide, and she looks down again. "Jesus, Shane. You're intense."

"You have no idea."

I look up at the sound of an engine, just in time to see Curt making his way over to us on an ATV.

"Hey, boss," he says when he cuts the engine. "Welcome home."

"Thanks. This is Ivie. Ivie, this is Curt."

"Ma'am." Curt offers her a nod. "Everything okay at the house?"

"It's great. Cox is coming this afternoon."

"He called me," Curt confirms. "He should arrive around oh-sixteen-hundred. Been quiet around here while you were gone."

"We like it quiet."

"So, Curt, how long have you lived here?" Ivie asks, trying to make conversation.

"Oh, going on about eight years or so now, I guess."

"Nice. And where are you from originally?"

Curt smiles politely but checks his watch. "I have some things to see to. Nice to meet you, ma'am."

He nods and takes off to the other side of the ranch.

"What did I say?"

"He doesn't like to talk about himself much."

"He's much younger than I expected," she admits. "You said he doesn't like to be around people?"

"No. He saw some bad things in action and has some pretty severe PTSD. He does better being a little isolated. The ranch suits him."

"Poor guy," she murmurs. "Okay, do I get to see this super-safe bunker?"

"Sure."

I lead her down the stairs to the large room below. I flip on lights and step to the side so she can look around.

"Holy shit, Shane. This is huge."

"Yeah." I grin and take it all in. "Tunnels run throughout the ranch. There's one to my house, Curt's cabin, the barn, and the helipad. All hidden from view, of course."

"Why are you showing me this?"

"I don't know, I think it's pretty cool."

She laughs and leads me through two bedrooms, a

bathroom, and the kitchen. "It *is* cool. Is this your toy? Like, some guys get expensive cars, and others like boats, but you have a crazy bunker?"

"Something like that, I guess."

She grins. "You really are 007."

I chuckle as she steps to me and drags her hands up my arms to my shoulders. Ivie's never been the aggressor, so I wait to see what she's got on her mind.

Those hands climb into my hair, and with her breasts pressed against me, she offers me her lips.

I won't turn down an offer this gorgeous.

This time, the kiss is sweet and slow but no less full of passion. I boost her up so she can wrap her legs around my waist and carry her to the wall so I can let my hands do a little wandering over her gorgeous curves.

She bites my bottom lip, making my already-hard dick jump in surprise.

"God, you're something." I nibble my way down her neck, enjoying the scent of lemons on her skin. "I want to fucking consume you."

"Three months of foreplay is a long time," she says and hums in satisfaction when my lips return to hers.

Barely holding myself in check, I yank her shirt out of her jeans and let my hand roam over the warm, smooth skin of her side and stomach before cupping her firm breast.

She arches into my hand in invitation.

"Find a bed," she instructs me. "We need more room, Shane. Somewhere softer."

"Right. A bed."

I carry her through a door to a small bedroom and tumble us both onto the unused mattress. No one has ever stayed down here.

Which means, we'll be christening this room.

I take the tab of her jeans in my teeth and yank the button free, and just as I start to urge them down her hips, my phone beeps.

"Damn it," I growl and look at the message. "I'm getting really sick and tired of being interrupted by technology."

"What is it?" Her voice is breathless, and her eyes are on fire.

"Cameron just landed."

"Oh, he has at least an hour until he's here, right?"

"No, sweetheart." I cover her again and kiss her softly. "He just landed on the helipad."

"Well, damn."

"Don't worry." I kiss her once more and then help us both to our feet. "The first time I have you isn't going to be in my bunker. It's going to be in *my* bed, where I can take my time and memorize every gorgeous inch of you."

"I'm going to hold you to that, Shane Martinelli."

I laugh and help her right herself. When we're both put back together, I kiss her temple. "Let's go put Cameron to work, shall we?"

"Oh, absolutely. I can't wait to see what he does to bring that thing back to life."

"He has tricks and secrets. He'll get it figured out, and then we'll know what your father was doing."

"I'm not sure I want to know."

"There's no going back now."

CHAPTER 6

"*N*ice to meet you," I say to a tall, dark, and ridiculously handsome Cameron Cox as the three of us walk from the helipad where Cameron just jumped out of a helicopter and to the house. "Is the pilot just going to wait there?"

"That's his job," Cameron says with a smile. "He'll be fine."

So, I guess he's not planning to stay, then.

"I didn't know helicopters could fly that far."

"We just had to stop in Boise to fuel up," Cameron replies as Shane opens the back door of the house, and we file inside. "So, your phone call was mysterious this morning."

"I'm hoping you can help us solve something." Shane unlocks the door to the basement, and we all go down the stairs.

Cameron has clearly been here before.

"Ivie has a flash drive that she needs to be able to read, and it's encrypted. When we tried to decode it, it wiped itself."

Cameron's eyebrows climb in surprise. "Interesting. Okay, let me see what I can do."

He sits behind the computer, and as it boots up, he slips black-rimmed glasses onto his nose and gets to work.

"Someone worked really hard to make sure this didn't get into the wrong hands," Cameron murmurs. "You have no idea what's on it?"

"None," I reply and watch in fascination as his fingers fly across the keys. When he taps out a series of numbers and letters in a formula I recognize, my eyebrows climb. "Oh, I never thought to do that."

"Why would you?" Cameron asks.

"Ivie's something of a computer hacker," Shane says with a proud grin. "It's a sight to behold."

"Really?" Cameron smiles at me. "That's pretty cool."

"How are things with that woman you were telling me about?" Shane asks him, making conversation. "Maggie?"

"Slow," Cameron mutters with a frown. "If anyone in the world is more stubborn than Mary Margaret O'Callaghan, I haven't met them. But I'm working on it. Okay, I've got it back."

"That was fast. Holy crap," I mutter.

"I'm good, sweetheart." He looks up at the screen. "Would you like me to translate this for you?"

"Absolutely." I drop into a chair beside him as he continues tapping the keyboard. Finally, words written in English fill the screen.

"Whoa," Cameron breathes. "This is some deep shit."

He clicks through some files and then turns to Shane.

"What is it?" Shane asks.

Cameron glances at me, but Shane just shakes his head. "It's *her* drive, man. She should know what it says."

Cameron blows out a breath and then starts in. "Okay, so this is all about a dude named Ivan Pavlov. I've heard of him. He died about a decade ago, in a really, *really* gnarly way. Anyway, this guy was a true piece of shit."

He stands to pace the room, and Shane and I turn to watch him. Shane's standing, his arms crossed over his chest. And all I can do is sit and listen to every single word.

"He was a European operative in the nineties. Ruthless. This man killed hundreds if not thousands of men, women, and children. Here."

He moves back to the computer and taps some keys. Suddenly, a folder with photographs opens.

"All of these photos are of people he killed, supposedly under the direction of his government. Although many think he was a mercenary and not tied to the government at all. Anyway, all of these people are dead because of him.

"Then, about twenty-five years ago or so, he got in with some extra-bad people. He pissed them off. Big time. And they said the only way to get back into their good graces—i.e., not get dead—was for him to kill his own family."

I feel Shane's eyes shift to me, but I can't take my eyes off of Cameron. How did I not know *any* of this?

He taps the keys, then stands to pace once more. Suddenly, I'm staring at a photo of my mother.

Murdered.

"He killed the wife," Cameron continues. "And as you can see, he wasn't nice about it. But I heard that he spared the kid because he decided he could get them—I don't know if it was a boy or a girl—to do his bidding. No one suspects a kid getting in and out of places. After he came to the US, Pavlov was mostly into selling information. As far as I know, he didn't kill here in the States like he did in Europe. Maybe he was getting older and wanted a new gig, who knows?"

"How do you know all of this?" Shane asks.

"I had to research him right before he died." Cameron turns to look at Shane. "I was on a team that had been given the order to find and terminate him, but someone beat us to it. It looks to me like every single sin this guy ever committed is documented on this drive, along with what looks like account numbers. Now, *my* question is, why do *you* have it?"

I can't stop staring at my mother. In the photo, her throat is slashed, her mouth open, her eyes staring in shock.

He killed her.

"They're my parents," I manage to say and then turn to look Cameron in the eyes. "I was the kid. And, yes, he used me. Ruthlessly. But I got away from the son of a bitch." I feel my blood boiling, running through my veins faster than ever before. And then I can't stand it anymore. I can't stay here.

I stand and flee, running up the stairs and through the house, then out the back door, just in time to lose whatever's in my stomach in the bushes beside the porch.

Someone comes up beside me, rubbing my back and holding my hair out of the way.

When it seems I have nothing left in me, I straighten, and Shane pulls me to him for a tight hug.

I don't even know how to process what I just saw. How do I deal with this?

"Hey, man, I have to get back to Seattle."

I clear my throat and turn to Cameron. "Thank you. Really. I appreciate your help. I'm going to let you two say goodbye. I'll be inside."

Cameron nods, and I hurry into the house and to the guest room, making a beeline for the bathroom so I can brush my teeth and wash my face.

But when I'm done, the anger and grief swamp me again.

My poor mama. My God, why did he do that to her?

"HERE, DRINK THIS," Shane says as he sets a cup of tea near my elbow. After Cameron left, Shane came inside, built a fire in the woodstove, and then set to work making me some tea. I just wrapped myself in a blanket and sat by the fire, staring at the pretty, orange flames.

"How could I not know?" I wonder aloud before taking a sip of the tea. "All of these years, I never knew the cause of my mother's death. He just came home one day and said she was dead and wasn't coming back."

I shake my head and wipe at a tear.

"I knew he was bad. I guess I didn't want to see that he was pure evil. He must have had that drive and wanted me to take it to someone to decrypt it for him. I don't know how he got it."

"But you never delivered it where he wanted it to go?"

"No." I shake my head and sip the tea. "I was so over it at that point, I hid it instead. I don't know why he would even have that. Basically, his resume of all the killing he did. Why would he have that?"

"I don't know how it came to be in his possession," Shane says, thinking it over. "Maybe they used it to blackmail him. If it got into the wrong hands, he could have been arrested and prosecuted. Maybe even deported to Bulgaria and executed."

"Oh my God," I gasp and stare at Shane in horror. "I should have called the police. All I did was run away. I should have called the police. It didn't even occur to me. How could I be so stupid?"

"Stop." Shane stands and joins me on the couch, pulling me to him. "You were a child."

"I was never really a child."

"Yes, you were. Despite what he made you do, you were still young, Ivie. You were just trying to survive. And I'd say you did a damn good job of that."

"He killed my mama." I feel the tears falling again and lean my head on his shoulder. "She was a good person. So funny. And she made the best breads and desserts. She would let me help her in the kitchen. Because *he* was gone so much, it was mostly just the two of us, hanging out together. We were already in the US when she died. She told me once that she was afraid of New York. It was so big, so noisy, and she didn't know the language very well."

"Do you speak Bulgarian?" he asks as he kisses my forehead.

"Not anymore. I did when I was very small but I don't remember it. I did everything I could to forget that life and to make this new one—one that doesn't embarrass me. I shouldn't just sit here and babble about my mother. She's been gone for a really long time."

"Yes, but for you, the wound is new again," he says. His voice is gentle and sexy at the same time. "You can talk about her. It's not like we have anywhere to be. I'd like to hear anything you want to say."

I kiss his cheek and smile up at him. "Thank you for always being so kind to me."

He wipes a tear from my cheek, and I think of my mother again.

"She was tall. Taller than my father. I must get my height from him, given how short I am." I smile a little as I think of her. "And she loved to dance."

For a long while, I just sit by the fire with this man I've come to care for, telling him the few stories I remember of my mother.

"I wish I knew more, but he never wanted to speak of her after she died."

I swallow and then something occurs to me.

"If those people want the drive, let's just give it to them, Shane. They'll have what they want. Although, at this point, I'm not sure it matters because he's dead and gone. I can just get on with my life."

He shifts and then shakes his head. "It's really not that simple."

"Why not?"

"After you came inside, Cameron and I had a minute to talk. He finished the story."

My stomach fills with dread. "What is it?"

"Well, there's no easy way to say this, so I'm just going to tell you. There's a bounty on your head, Ivie. One million dollars for your capture—dead or alive."

"The *police* want me dead?"

"No, baby, not the police. Those bad guys Cameron told us about. They're still pissed at your father. And it's not just one group. Apparently, this goes deep. The man who took you the other day has likely been looking for you for a very long time. He was going to kill you and collect the money. Just as any of them would."

"*Why?*" And then that man's words come back to me. "To pay for the sins of my father."

"These guys have a long memory," Shane says quietly. "They're worse than the mafia, and that's saying a lot given what my family is capable of. I'd like to know what your father did to them to make them this angry."

"I have no idea. He might have killed someone he wasn't supposed to or stole from someone and really pissed them off. He couldn't hang on to money to save his life. Who knows?"

"Well, one thing I do know is that we're staying here for a while. We're safest here. I'm going to start doing some digging, and Cameron said he'd do some on his end, as well. I'm supposed to meet up with him in Denver in a week."

"You don't pass information via the internet." It's not a question.

"No. Not this kind. It's too sensitive. He'll bring anything he uncovers with him next week. In the meantime, I'll put out the word that my associates should keep their eyes and ears open, and I'll work on the secure network downstairs."

"I can probably help with that."

"If I need you, I'll let you know. But I want your fingers out of this as much as possible."

"So, what? I'm just supposed to *sit* here for God knows how long?" I stare at him with disgust. "I'm not good at being idle, Shane."

"You won't be. We're going to start some lessons."

"What kind?"

"I'm going to teach you to shoot. We'll go over hand-to-hand. You're going to learn to defend yourself if anything like this were to happen again."

"Have you *met* me? I'm the clumsiest person on Earth. I have no business holding a gun."

"You're going to shake that and get used to it. You're going to be so good by the time I'm done with you, being clumsy won't even be a thought in your beautiful head."

I blink up at him. "Really?"

"Really. You'll never be taken by surprise like that again."

"You're intense. I kind of like it."

"For today, just relax. Take a nap if you want. I'm going to start making those calls."

"A nap actually sounds really nice." I stand and stretch. "I'll go lie down."

I walk to the guest room, but Shane calls out my name.

"You won't be sleeping in there. You'll sleep with me. Go have a nap in my room."

I grin at him, but he's already looking down at his phone. So, I change course, shuck my jeans and socks, maneuver my way out of my bra, and then climb under the cool, crisp sheets.

His bed is comfortable, and my eyes are heavy from all of the crying.

Finally, I fall asleep.

No! Don't you dare do that!

"Shut up." Father slaps me aside and turns to Shane, who's kneeling on the floor. My father fists Shane's hair and pulls his head back, ready to slice his throat with a knife.

"No!" I try to run at him again, but my feet won't move. I can't get to him. Oh my God, I can't move! "Don't kill him! Please, don't. No."

"Shh." Shane cradles me to him. "Just a dream, baby."

"He was going to kill you." I grip onto him tightly and bury my face against his chest. "Oh, God, he was going to kill you. Just like he did my mama."

"I'm right here, and he's long-dead, Ivie. He can't hurt me."

I can't stop the tears. They just keep coming. For

my poor mama and the thought of losing Shane in the same way.

"He can't hurt me," he says again and kisses the top of my head.

"But he keeps hurting me," I whisper and shake my head in despair. "He keeps hurting me."

CHAPTER 7

"You have a shooting range."

It's the following morning, and I'm pleased to see that the shadows have cleared from Ivie's eyes this morning. After a quick breakfast, I brought the sexiest woman alive to my own private little playground, out here in the middle of nowhere.

It's a bit overkill, as Carmine would say. But it keeps me in top form. I have to practice and work on my skills so I don't get killed on the job.

"Yes, I do." I press my palm to a plate to unlock the door with my print, and the door slides open. I flip a switch, and lights illuminate the massive area that I carved into the side of the mountain.

"Holy shit, Shane, this is some crazy high-tech stuff," she says. "I thought this only existed in movies."

"If you have the money and know the right people, it's out there."

"And you know the right people. You're a little scary. Also, this was just a door in the side of a hill," she reminds me.

"Actually, once upon a time, this was a gold mine. Gold is huge up here in the mountains, and just about five miles that way,"—I point to the west—"is a mine that yields several million dollars in gold every day. This particular shaft has been abandoned for a hundred years at least. When I bought the property, I knew it would be the perfect place to hollow out and put in my shooting range."

"Of course." She nods, then glances around with her hands on her hips. "That's what I would think when I see an abandoned mine. *Let's make it into a super-secret, high-tech shooting range.*"

"Precisely." I laugh at her sarcasm and pull her to me for a quick kiss, then lead her to another door before I decide to press her against the wall and take her right there in the side of a mountain. "Lay your hand right here."

She frowns but does as I ask. I tap on the screen of my phone, recording her palm print into the security system. When the light blinks green, another door slides open.

"You have access to this door now," I say as more lights flip on and we step inside.

"Holy. Shit." She stops and turns in a circle, taking

in the weapons lining the walls around us. I'm fully equipped with everything a person could ever need—especially if they're going to war. "It's an arsenal."

"Yes." I take a deep breath as she turns back to me and stares up at me with confused blue eyes.

"Who the hell are you, Shane?"

"It's better if you don't know the answer to that." I take her hand and walk her to the back of the vault where the bulk of my handguns are stored behind glass in a case mounted to the wall. The ammunition is kept beneath the case in a stainless-steel cabinet. "We're starting out small and easy. This is a .22 pistol. It won't have much kickback, and it will fit easily in your hands."

I take the weapon from behind the glass and offer it to her.

"Shane—"

"It's not loaded yet. I want you to hold it. Get a feel for the weight of it, how it feels in your palm. A weapon should be an extension of your hand. It's a tool."

She does as I ask, careful not to point the barrel at herself or me.

"This isn't your first rodeo." My voice is full of surprise as I watch her hold the weapon with the hands of someone who's done it many times before.

"I took a class once," she says softly. "But it made me nervous because I *am* so clumsy. I always worried that I'd hurt someone."

"You didn't have confidence," I reply and retrieve two boxes of ammo for the gun, then take her hand and lead her to the firing range. "Which tells me that whomever you took the class from was shitty at their job."

"Maybe. I was one of about twenty students."

"I'm not shitty at this," I inform her as I set up a target, then flip a switch and send the paper with its black outline down the lane about twenty yards. "In fact, it might be one of the things I'm best at. And we can practice as long as it takes to get you comfortable. I want this to be as easy as breathing for you."

"We could be here a while," she says with a laugh.

"I have time." I kiss her cheek, then reach for two sets of eye and ear protection. "Okay, we're going to start simple. Are you ready?"

"As I'll ever be."

"For this round, I'll load and get you ready to go. But after this, you'll do it. We'll also practice doing it quickly. The bad guys won't wait for you to load a gun."

"I feel like I'm in boot camp," she mutters, making me laugh.

"Nah. We're much more friendly here." I load the magazine with rounds of ammo, clip it into the gun, and pass it to Ivie. "Here we go."

I step back to watch her first, to see how much she already knows. Her stance is excellent, feet spread shoulder-width apart, her hands wrapped around the gun, her shoulders down.

Damn, she looks like a fucking pro.

When she empties the magazine, she turns to me.

"I don't buy that you didn't do well in that class."

She shrugs a shoulder. "I didn't say I didn't do well. I just didn't feel comfortable."

"Okay, let's build that confidence."

"How do you feel?" I ask her after we lock up the range and head toward the barn.

"I'm okay," she says.

"Does anything hurt?"

"My hands are tired. Who knew that squeezing a trigger that much could wear out your hands?"

I knew. But I keep the thought to myself.

"We have one more stop this morning."

"Are we feeding animals?" she asks as I park by the barn.

"No. I don't have much for animals here. Just some elk, deer, and the occasional mountain lion or bear." I wink at her, and we walk toward the barn door, which is also secured with a palm plate.

"It feels like your security might be overkill."

I turn and look at her, then bust up laughing. "That's exactly what Carmine says."

"Your brother's not wrong."

"The security is necessary. And right now, I'm damn glad I have it to keep *you* safe. Come on."

We walk inside, and I'm pleased to see that Curt is already here.

I converted the barn into a massive gym about five years ago. On this floor, we have a sparring ring and weights. The second floor has treadmills, ellipticals, rowing machines, and bikes.

"You don't do anything half-assed, do you?" Ivie asks, turning to me.

"No, ma'am. What's the point in that? Or the fun?" I cross to Curt, who's already dressed in a simple T-shirt and gym shorts. "Thanks for doing this."

"Hey, I just work here," he says with a half-smile.

"What are we doing?" Ivie asks, her brow raised.

"Sparring."

She coughs in surprise and then stares at the two of us. "The two of you are going to beat each other up? Why do I have to be here for this?"

"No, honey. You and Curt are going to spar. I'm going to coach you."

She looks back and forth between us. "You're insane."

"That may be true, but it doesn't change things. Now, let's step into the ring."

"No." Ivie crosses her arms over her chest. "I'm not *hitting* anyone."

"Let me ask you something." I don't walk to her, just stand my ground and fist my hands at my sides. "If you'd had some self-defense training, would that asshole have been able to take you out of the office like that? Would he have been able to stick that syringe into you and just walk you out of there?"

"I don't—"

"No. The answer to that is *no*. Now, we're going to make sure that no one has the opportunity to do that again, Ivie. And this is part of that."

"I don't want to punch Curt. He's too nice for that."

"No," Curt says with a shake of his head. "I'm not. I probably have it coming, Miss Ivie."

"You're Southern," she says. "Where are—?"

"Let's do this," Curt interrupts and walks into the ring, deflating Ivie's sails.

"I'm going to break through that wall he's got up," she says to me as she stomps past. "Mark my words."

I just shake my head and follow behind her, enjoying the way her hips sway when she's riled up.

Ivie certainly has less experience with hand-to-hand than she does firing a gun. We spend an hour just going over the basics.

She's sweaty and panting when I give her the order to go ahead and punch Curt in the face.

"No." She turns to me in horror. "I'm not going to actually punch him."

"Yes, you are."

"It's okay," Curt assures her. "You can't hurt me."

Ivie's eyes narrow at the challenge, and I see determination fill them as she takes the stance we've been teaching her, stomps on his foot, then follows through with a right hook to the jaw, sending Curt back on his ass.

"Oh, yeah?" Ivie asks, staring down at him.

"Okay, I was wrong." He cradles his jaw in his hand and shifts it back and forth. "That hurt. Nice one, Miss Ivie."

"Thanks." She grins and offers her hand to help him off the floor.

But Curt doesn't like to be touched, so he just shakes his head and climbs to his feet unassisted.

"One more time," Curt says.

"I really don't want to hit you again," Ivie says and turns pleading eyes to me. "Don't make me."

"You're too nice," Curt says and approaches her from behind. Wrapping his arm around her neck, Ivie immediately slips into defensive mode. She slips out of his hold, knees him in the balls, and jams the heel of her hand into his nose, making it bleed. "Never mind. Not too nice."

"Oh, God." Ivie covers her face with her hands. "I'm so sorry."

"You did exactly what you were supposed to do," Curt says and dabs at his nose. "I provoked you on purpose. A few more lessons, and you'll be able to kick both our asses with a blindfold on."

Ivie's smile is wide and proud. "Yeah?"

"Yeah," Curt replies. "Good job."

"Why won't Curt talk about himself?" Ivie asks when we walk into the house, and I start making us sandwiches for a late lunch.

"I told you, he has some baggage. He doesn't like to be around people."

"He can't be more than thirty-five," she says.

"What does his age have to do with anything?"

She shrugs and bites into a potato chip. "I don't know. It just seems sad. He's so young."

I stop opening the mayo and slowly turn to her. "Ivie, are you telling me that you have a crush on my ranch manager?"

She scowls and then laughs. "No. No, *he's* not the one I have a crush on at all. I just feel bad for him because he seems kind. And he's young and handsome and—"

"If you keep singing Curt's praises, I'll fire him."

She laughs in earnest and crosses over to me. She wraps her arms around my middle and lays her cheek on my chest. "I just like him. And maybe I feel bad for him."

"Don't." I kiss the top of her head. "He's where he wants to be, doing what he loves."

She sighs and then tips her face up to mine. "I'm glad you're his friend. I'm hungry."

"If you stop singing Curt's praises, I'll finish making lunch."

She grins. "Deal."

She pulls another handful of chips out of the bag

and munches happily as she watches me build sandwiches.

"Are we ever going to have sex?"

The turkey falls out of my hand and onto the counter as I spin and stare at her. "What?"

"Sex. You and me. Is it ever going to happen, or are we just going to flirt and kiss and drive me crazy forever? I just want to know so I can plan accordingly."

"What if the answer is no sex?"

She shrugs. "Then I need to order a vibrator or something because a girl can't be with a sexy guy like you forever and not touch the goods. Is that how it's going to be?"

"Fuck, no." I shake my head and return to the sandwiches. "You were a little upset last night, Ivie. And we had things to do this morning."

"So, you're a planner when it comes to sex."

I cut the sandwiches and deliver them to the breakfast bar. She immediately digs into hers as if we're discussing the stock market. I take a bite, as well.

"I didn't say that."

"You just said—"

"I know what I said. And it didn't include *plans* for sex. It just wasn't...shit, I don't know. I want you so badly that I ache with it. I've wanted you naked and under me the minute I saw you at Annika's wedding, for Christ's sake. Keeping my hands to myself has been the hardest thing I've ever done."

"Cool. Let's not do that anymore, okay?"

"Do what?"

"Keep our hands to ourselves. I'm sleeping in *your* bed. I haven't told you no, and I don't plan to. I'm on the pill, I'm healthy, and I want you, Shane. I'm not playing games here. This also isn't a Stockholm syndrome thing. I'd want you under *any* circumstance. So now you know."

"Are you about done with that sandwich?"

She grins and sets it on the plate. "Yeah."

"Good."

I circle the breakfast bar and take her face in my hands, staring down into her fierce, blue eyes. "If there's anything you *don't* like, you need to tell me."

"I'm not shy, and I don't think you could do much that I won't like."

"Jesus, I don't deserve you." I kiss her long and hard and then take her hands and pull her quickly through the house to my bedroom. I close and lock the door.

"Expecting someone?" she asks.

"I'm not taking any damn chances." I shuck my boots and yank my shirt over my head. "Now that I have you here, right where I want you, I'm not taking any chances that someone could fuck this up."

"Good plan." She smiles and pulls the band out of her ponytail, setting her hair free, letting it tumble around her shoulders. Then, she calmly pulls her pink shirt over her head and lets it fall to the floor. With her eyes on mine, she unclasps her bra from the front and drops it with the shirt.

I swallow hard. Jesus fucking Christ, she's gorgeous. Those full breasts that I can't wait to get my hands on are on full display, her nipples already tight and begging for my lips.

When she reaches for the waistband of her yoga pants, I shake my head once and then step forward.

"Let me," I whisper as I take her hand in mine and draw it up to my lips. "Let me unwrap the rest of you. I'm going to worship every damn inch of your gorgeous body."

"It's good, then, that I have lots of extra inches for you to enjoy." Her lips twitch, in both humor and a little insecurity.

"Every bit of you is stunning. And I'm going to show you, slowly and methodically, just how much I want you. All of you. Every bit."

"Oh, that sounds like a good idea."

CHAPTER 8

*H*as anyone ever looked at me the way Shane's gazing at me right now? Like he wants to eat me with a spoon?

No. The answer to that would be a resounding *no*.

"Are you getting nervous on me?" he asks as he slowly crosses to me and hooks his finger into the waistband of my yoga pants.

"No, why do you ask?"

"Because I can see your pulse throbbing, right here." He leans in and ever-so-gently lays his lips over the tender flesh of my neck. If I wasn't already turned on, which I definitely am, that would have done the trick. He's warm, and when my hands glide up his bare arms, he's smooth and firm. And I get to touch him. Do whatever I want to and with him.

Good God, am I dreaming?

"It's not because I'm nervous." I swallow hard and let my eyes drift closed as pure sensation floats through me.

"No?"

I slowly shake my head and then smile when his lips drift up to my jawline and over to my lips.

This kiss isn't light, playful, or comforting.

It's slow and hot. Arousing. All-encompassing.

"Never met anyone quite like you," he whispers as his hands slip into my pants, and he slowly pushes them over my hips. He makes a sweet, slow journey down my torso with his lips, planting hot kisses as he guides my pants down my legs.

When I'm standing before him in nothing but my neon green panties, he kisses me over the small scrap of material, right on my pubis.

My sharp inhale of breath has his gaze flying up to mine, and with an amused grin, he stands, takes my hand, and leads me to the bed.

Shane's eyes are soft and so full of lust, it makes me want to look behind myself to make sure it's *me* he's gazing at.

The thought makes me laugh a little.

"Is this funny?"

"No."

With his hands framing my face, he urges me onto the mattress and rolls me to the middle of the bed where he can cover me and keep kissing me.

"What made you smile?"

"Just a stupid thought."

"None of your thoughts are stupid, Ivie."

I love that he calls me Ivie. That it seemingly never even occurred to him to use my given name when he learned the truth about me.

"Just trust me on this," I assure him and push my fingers through his dark hair. "You still have your pants on."

His lips twitch. "What are you going to do about it?"

I bite my lip, considering, then push against his shoulder and urge him back, reversing our positions.

I've never been quite so bold in all my life, but it's exhilarating to be the one in control—if only for a few moments.

Rather than tug his jeans open with my hands, I kiss down the hard ridges of his abs, nuzzle his navel, and grip the denim with my teeth, pulling the top button free. All five open easily, and I'm not even a little surprised to find him naked underneath.

"I guess that answers that question."

"Which one is that?" He gently pushes his fingers through my hair.

"Boxers or briefs?"

He snorts out a laugh but smothers it when I urge his jeans over his hips and plant a kiss on his cock, right under his sensitive tip. Shane's hips jerk in surprise. When his jeans are long gone, I don't give him time to retake control.

I take his cock in my hand and wrap my lips around the tip, enjoying myself.

He's rock-hard, and if the way he moves beneath me, and the moans of delight coming from his lips are to be believed, he's enjoying my efforts immensely.

"Jesus H., Ivie, where did you learn to do that?"

Satisfaction bubbles through me, but suddenly, he rears up, takes my shoulders in his hands, and pushes me back onto the bed.

"Hey, I was having fun."

"Too much fun. I'm not going to come in your mouth the first time. We're going to make this last a bit."

"Okay, I'll do it again later."

He laughs and kisses me hard. "Do you have any idea how fucking beautiful you are?"

I raise a brow. "I'm glad you think so."

I'm not stupid. I know I'm not a beauty queen. I'm passable at best. But it fills my heart with joy that this sexy-as-hell man thinks I'm attractive.

His lips are everywhere. His movements are suddenly more urgent as if he just can't hold himself back any longer.

And I don't want him to. I want Shane to lose himself in me. In *us*. I don't think he lets himself just *feel* very often. The fact that he's doing so with me is both humbling and arousing.

He doesn't guide my underwear down my legs.

No, he just rips them off.

I blink at him in surprise.

"They were in my way." With that simple statement, he nudges my legs apart with his shoulders and settles in between them.

But he doesn't lower his mouth to me.

He *pets* me.

His fingers linger over my lips, then glide up to my clit, barely pass over it, and then move back down again.

My hips surge.

"Lord, have mercy," I mutter as my back arches. "Shane."

"Yes, baby?"

"Shane."

"I'm right here."

"More."

He kisses the inside of my thigh. "What do you need? Tell me."

"More," I repeat and reach blindly to grip the sheets.

"More of this?" His touch is firmer now, but it's not his fingers I want. "Or this?" He gently circles my hard clit—electricity shooting through me. "What do you want?"

"You." The word is a plea. My God, I feel like I'm about to burst from wanting him. "Your mouth."

"Good girl. Watch this."

I open my eyes and watch as he lowers his head to lick me. Then, he starts doing magical things that I can't even comprehend as my head falls back against the pillow, and he treats my body to a smorgasbord of sensation.

I can't hold back. I couldn't if I wanted to. Falling over the crest of oblivion is as natural as water rushing over a waterfall.

And when I begin to surface, I feel those magical lips on my thighs, then up my belly. When he buries his face against my neck and takes a long, deep breath, I wrap myself around him, arms and legs enfolding him, needing him close.

"I'm clean, too," he whispers against my ear. "I'd never put you at risk."

"I know."

And with that invitation, with his face close to mine, and our bodies twined together, he slowly slips inside me, filling me completely.

"Christ," he mutters, his voice hoarse. "Christ, Ivie."

I stroke his back, his hand slipping beneath me to cup my ass as he begins to move. He does so slowly at first and then with vigor, the push and pull driving us both over that cliff and into the abyss beyond.

When the room quiets, and we're tangled together, both catching our breath, I smile and drag my foot up his calf. "I've been waiting for that for months. I didn't think you'd ever want to do me."

He snorts. "You have such a fun way with words." He turns his head to press a kiss to my cheek. "I've enjoyed getting to know you. It's unexpected and not typical for me, but the learning-you parts, the *foreplay* as you put it, has been as fun as the sex itself. And given that I can't feel my legs and am eighty-percent sure I had a stroke when I came, that's saying something."

I can't help the giggle that comes out of me, and I drag my fingertips down his cheek.

I'm in love with him. I've been falling for weeks. Every time he called me, each time we flirted during a meal or just exchanged looks from across a room, led to this.

Shane Martinelli is everything I've ever hoped to find in a man. Not because he completes me or anything cliché like that, but because he's simply...*him.* I know he thinks we can't have anything permanent because of his dangerous job.

But maybe he'll come around. Perhaps he'll see how good we are together and change his mind.

I CAN'T SLEEP. I've never had insomnia issues before, and after a rigorous afternoon of sex, some delicious food, and even *more* sex, you'd think I'd be comatose.

Shane's sleeping soundly next to me, his breaths even as the light of the moon filters through the window.

I envy him. I'm restless, so rather than toss and turn next to him, potentially waking him, I slip from the bed and wrap up in one of his flannel shirts. I'm able to get out the door without a sound and decide I'd like to sit outside.

We're headed solidly into fall, and evenings are cool here in the mountains, so I grab a blanket off the couch on my way to the back door.

It's a clear night. With no light noise from any city, it's *dark*, aside from the light of the moon, and I can see more stars than I ever have in my life.

If I'm not mistaken, I can see Venus. I bundle the blanket around me and take a long, deep breath of crisp, fresh air.

I see why Shane loves it out here. The air is clean, and no one's around.

I would never have thought I'd enjoy the quiet like this, but it's peaceful.

A coyote howls in the distance. A light breeze blows through, rustling the bushes beside the back porch.

I can see Curt's little cabin off in the distance. The lights are on, and there's a small trail of smoke coming from a chimney. I can't help but wonder what kind of horrors that man has seen in his life to make him want to exile himself out here with no interaction with anyone except Shane. Did the two of them serve together? Did they see the same horrors? Neither seems eager to discuss it.

But I'm nosy, and I'm curious.

An owl—at least, I think it's an owl—flies overhead, making me smile. It may be quiet, but it's not boring out here, even at night.

I don't know exactly what has me so restless tonight. "I'm just silly."

"Hoo. Hoo."

I glance up. Yep, it's an owl.

"I am," I reply with a smile. "I should be fast asleep, and you should be out hunting for your breakfast."

"Hoo. Hoo."

"Exactly."

Suddenly, there's a commotion behind me, and Shane comes running out the back door, yelling my name.

"Ivie! Ivie!"

"Hey, I'm right here." I stand, letting the blanket fall. "Shane, I'm right here."

He's panting and out of breath as his chin falls to his chest in relief, and then he takes my shoulders in his hands. "Don't ever fucking do that again."

"Do what? I couldn't sleep so I came out to look at the stars."

"You can't just leave while I'm asleep and not tell me where you're going."

"Yes. I can."

He shakes his head and paces away from me as if he's completely frustrated. "No, Ivie. There are people out there looking for you. People who want you *killed*. And it's my goddamn job to keep you safe. I can't do that when I don't know where you are."

"Where am I going to go?" I demand and prop my hands on my hips, staring at him. "You're overreacting,

Shane. I couldn't sleep so I came out to talk to that owl that just flew off. I didn't sneak out to go to a party."

"I'm not overreacting." He shakes his head and then rubs the back of his neck in agitation. "I woke up, and you were gone. Not in the bathroom, not grabbing something in the kitchen. *Gone.* I have top-of-the-line security here. If anyone breached the perimeter, I have alarms that would go off. But what if someone managed to slip through and get you?"

"Hey, they didn't." I walk toward him, but he won't let me touch him. "Shane, I literally just wanted some fresh air."

"Just wake me up and tell me next time." He blows out a breath.

"You're scared." I blink at him in surprise.

"Of course, I am." He rubs his hand over his mouth. "You'll never know what it felt like to hear that you'd been taken. To watch the footage on Annika's tape. To know that someone had you and I wasn't there to get you."

"But you did get me."

He shakes his head. "You don't get it."

"Okay, tell me."

He rubs his neck again. This time, I don't let him back away. I wrap my arms around him and press my cheek to his chest.

"Tell me." My voice is quiet now.

"If something happened to you, I don't know that I would ever get over it." He presses his lips to my head.

"You are important, Ivie. I won't ever let someone get to you again. If you want fresh air, we'll get fresh air. But I need to *know*."

"Okay." I rub his back in soothing circles. "I'm sorry that I scared you. I just wanted to let you sleep."

"When all of this is over, you can let me sleep."

Is he still going to be around when all this is finished?

It's a question I'm not brave enough to ask. Not yet.

"So, if I want to go for a walk on your property, I have to ask for permission?"

"Either Curt or I will go with you."

"Okay." I kiss his chest and pull back to look up at him. "I have to use the bathroom. Do you want to go with me to that, too?"

His lips twitch as his eyes narrow into slits. "Wouldn't bother me a bit."

I scowl. "Ew. It would bother *me*. You aren't allowed in the bathroom. That's where I draw the line."

"We all have one," he says simply. "Do you still want to sit out here?"

"The owl and I are done talking." I reach down for the blanket. "We can go in. I'm sorry you ended up waking up anyway."

"I'm not. You scared ten years off my life, and I have a feeling it's going to be a short one as it is."

I stop and stare up at him. "Don't say stuff like that." He shrugs and moves to walk inside, but I stop him. "Seriously. Don't. You hate the idea of something happening to me, and the same goes for me, Shane. It's not funny."

"No." He kisses my nose and then takes the blanket to carry. "You're right, it's not funny. Let's go get some rest."

CHAPTER 9

"Holy crap, I'm sweaty," Ivie says as we hop off the ATV and walk toward the house. "That was quite a workout."

"You did more than I expected." I take her hand and smile down at her, proud of her. She kicked ass today. Literally. "I think Curt will need a long soak in a hot bath. It's a good thing I provide him with excellent health insurance."

"I don't like hitting him," she says softly. "I'm not a violent person like my father was."

"I know." We stop on the porch, in the same place we stood last night, and I kiss her forehead. "But you have to practice. You didn't hit him much. I'm just teasing you."

"I don't like hitting at all. And carrying a gun around in my pants isn't my favorite thing, either."

"It won't be forever. Just until we get this mess all figured out."

She sighs and then nods. "I don't mean to complain. Thank you for everything you're doing for me. I'm gonna go hop in the shower and get this ick off me."

"Enjoy it. I'll be in in just a bit."

She walks into the house, and I pull my phone out of my pocket. I dial Carmine's number and wait for him to answer.

"Yo," he says in greeting.

"How are things there?" I ask, getting straight to the point.

"Quiet. Rocco and I are in the office, and we were just saying that it's been very quiet. No chatter."

"That's not typical." I lean on the railing and watch a herd of elk make their way into my pasture about a hundred yards away. "I don't like it when it's quiet."

"I know. The ears on the ground say the same thing. No chatter, pretty mellow right now."

"That means something's going to happen."

"We agree," Rocco says, clearly on speakerphone. "You're right to stay there for now. It's likely the safest place."

"Agreed," I say with a sigh. Not because I don't like being on my ranch. Quite the opposite. It's the safest place for us, and it's where I feel the most comfortable. But I don't like this quiet. Feeling on edge, like the other shoe is about to drop. "I'm waiting for more info from Cox, and I have some feelers out, but I'm trying to be inconspicuous. It takes time."

"If you need us, we can be there in a couple of hours. Or you can always come here if need be," Carmine reminds me. "I know you don't think it's as safe as the ranch, but we can lock it down when we need to."

"I know. Thanks. I'll check in tomorrow."

"Over and out," Rocco says, cutting off the call.

Like I said, I don't like it when there's no chatter. It's like when a person has a toddler, and quiet means chaos.

For now, all I can do is what I'm already doing. So, I walk inside, expecting Ivie to be out of the shower by now.

But when I come around the corner, I hear her talking to someone. I slow down, listening.

"I will fuck you up. That's right, I said it. You don't want a piece of me. Oh, does that make you nervous? What are you going to do about it?"

I inch forward, wanting to get a glimpse of what's going on without being seen. If someone's in there with her, I'll kill them.

I pull my sidearm from the holster at my back and continue inching forward.

"Are you looking at me?"

I peer around the door and feel every muscle loosen in relief. Ivie's standing in front of the mirror in just her blue jeans and black bra, her pistol tucked into her jeans at the small of her back. She quickly whips it out and points it at herself in the mirror.

"Are you fucking looking at *me?*" she demands and narrows her eyes at herself, leaning forward. "Yeah, that's what I thought."

Then she holsters her weapon again.

I have to clamp my hand over my mouth so I don't bust up laughing. I wouldn't miss this show for the world.

She starts to walk away, then turns back quickly, drawing the weapon once more.

"Don't piss me off, asshole."

I can't help it anymore. I can't hold in the laughter. Ivie stills, and I see her cringe in the mirror as I walk up behind her and rest my hands on her shoulders, looking her reflection in the eyes.

"You're kind of scary."

She presses her lips into a line as her cheeks bloom into a bright pink. I want to kiss the hell out of her.

"I didn't know you were there."

"Obviously." I grin and kiss her neck where it meets her shoulder. "You do a great DeNiro impression."

"You weren't supposed to see that. Besides, you're the one who literally just told me that I need to practice drawing my weapon."

"I did, you're completely right." I can't keep my hands off her. She's simply irresistible. She spins to face me, and our lips meet in a kiss that starts sweet but quickly escalates to hot and needy.

"I'm too sweaty for sex," she informs me but doesn't push me away when I free her of her bra and let it fall to the floor.

"You're just going to get sweaty again."

"It's different," she insists and presses her hands to my chest. "Seriously, I need to wash up."

"Okay." I kiss her once more, then back up. "I'll help."

She quirks a brow. "Will you?"

"I'm an excellent back-washer," I inform her, keeping my expression perfectly serious. "I've been told that I should go into business for myself, washing backs."

"Told by whom?" She quirks a brow, purses her lips, and I know this is a trap.

Well, shit.

"Uh…"

She laughs and slips around me to start the water in the shower. "Relax, Shane. You're no virgin. Neither am I, actually."

I frown. I don't like the thought of Ivie having had sex with anyone but me. I know the way she sounds, the way her fists clench in the sheets—or my hair. The way she tastes.

And the fact that *anyone* in the past or the future would have the same knowledge fills me with an all-consuming rage.

"Why do you look like that?" she asks.

"Like what?"

"Like you want to punch a wall."

I make myself grin and then shrug. "I couldn't tell you."

She doesn't smile back. She just blinks at me, and then, before stepping into the shower, hits me with, "Don't lie to me again, Martinelli."

I catch her elbow before she can step into the shower. "I don't like the thought of other men having been with you."

She nods once. "That's better. And I don't like the idea of you washing someone else's back. But, we're both old enough to know that we've been with other people. That doesn't mean I'm sleeping with anyone else now. And for as long as you're having sex with *me*, I'd ask for the same consideration."

I love the fire in her blue eyes. She's staking a claim, here and now. And as much as I've told myself over and over again that this can't go anywhere, that even though I'm completely wrapped up in her, she can never really be mine, I can't help but feel my gut clench, and my heart pound in response to her possessiveness.

"Baby, I can't *see* anyone but you." I cup her cheek and bend down to kiss her softly. "Now, let's get in this shower before we waste all the hot water."

"Do these still hurt?" I brush my fingertips over her damp skin where the bruises over her ribs have turned from black to green. I reach for some arnica and rub it gently over the wounded area.

"No, they're just ugly now," she says and then sighs at my touch. "You're good with your hands. And now I can vouch for the back-washing praise. You're hired."

I grin as I turn to wash my hands, and Ivie pulls her clothes on.

"Shane?"

"Yeah."

"I'm bored." She leans on the vanity and crosses her arms over her chest. "I'm getting cabin fever."

I walk into the closet to put on clean clothes, and Ivie follows me.

"Let's go somewhere."

"No."

"*Shane.*" It's not a whine, but it's damn close. "We've been in this house for almost a week. And while I love your ranch, I need to see something else."

"And you will. As soon as—"

"As soon as we figure this out," she finishes for me. "Let's just go for a drive. Just a short one where I can see different trees. Your windows are tinted, and no one's up here anyway. We're in the middle of nowhere."

I should stick to my guns and say no, but she's been restless all morning, and I know she's not a loner like I am.

"We could drive into town and get lunch at the best

deli I've ever been to," I offer. "But you have to stay in the car when I pick it up."

"Deal." She hops and claps her hands in excitement. "Perfect."

"I'll call ahead and order," I mutter. "But don't get used to this."

"Of course." She crosses her heart and holds her fingers up like she's a Boy Scout. "Scouts' honor."

"You were never a Boy Scout."

She giggles. "Well, no. But I promise. Thank you. I'm going to grab my shoes."

She runs out, and I send a text to Curt, filling him in. Then I call the deli to place an order. Ten minutes later, we're in my SUV and headed into town, which is only about twenty minutes away.

"The trees are turning," she murmurs. "I bet it's gorgeous up here in the fall."

"Another week, and it'll be breathtaking."

She bites her lip, and I reach out to take her hand. "We might still be here."

She nods.

"You're always welcome here, Ivie, whether assholes are chasing you or not."

That makes her smile, and she glances my way. "Is there a private spot where you can pull over?"

"Do you have to pee or something?"

She just smiles again, so I pull over to the side of the road. "This is private. It's still my property."

"Geez, Shane, how much land did you buy?"

"A thousand acres."

She blinks over at me in surprise. Once I've put the vehicle in park, she unbuckles her belt and leans over the center console.

Her hands dive for my jeans.

"Here?" My voice is high and breaks as if I'm a fifteen-year-old kid.

"Here." But she doesn't climb on top of me, she takes my cock in her hand, jacks me twice, and then sinks that sweet mouth of hers over the head. I'm immediately lost to her.

"Fucking hell, Ivie."

The woman is a master with her mouth and with her hands.

I push the seat back so she has more room, and so I can lean back a bit and enjoy the ride. She never fails to surprise me. And just now, as she cups my balls and sucks gently, I see stars.

"Jesus." It's a prayer and a curse, and before I can stop myself, I'm coming. I watch as Ivie laps up every drop, then sits back, buckles her belt, and wipes her mouth.

"Well, that was fun."

I bark out a laugh as I tuck myself away. "What did I do to deserve that?"

"You're taking me for a drive," she says simply. "And I appreciate it."

"You're easy to please, sweetheart."

"Not really." She shrugs as I put the vehicle in gear

and start once more toward town. "But you're irresistible."

My eyes narrow into slits as we get closer to town. I survey the streets, looking for anything out of place, but it looks the same as it always does. Like it's something out of the Old West.

"Wow, it's like a time capsule," she says, echoing my thoughts.

"It was a booming gold town about a hundred years ago," I inform her. "When it seemed that most of the gold had been mined, people left to find other claims. Some stayed. There's always been working mines here, but it slowed down considerably. The downtown area looks pretty much the same as it did back in the old days. The buildings have withstood the test of time."

"It's very cool," she says. "I'd love to wander around and take it all in."

"Another time. I promise. Today, I'm anxious to grab lunch and get back to the ranch."

"I understand." I glance over when she lays her hand on my arm. "Honest, I do."

"Good." I park right in front of the deli. "Lock these doors. Do you have your weapon?"

"Of course."

"Keep it handy. Keep your eyes open. Don't look at your phone or fall asleep."

"You'll be gone for all of thirty seconds," she reminds me.

"Sometimes, that's all it takes." I lean over and kiss her cheek. "Do as I say."

"Yes, sir."

I hop out of the car and nod in satisfaction when I hear the snick of the locks. Ivie isn't careless, and I know she'll do as I ask.

"Well, good morning, handsome."

Mrs. Ullrich is sixty-five if she's a day, and she's a hopeless flirt. She's also been married for forty-seven years and has eight children, some of whom are my age.

"Hey there, Mrs. Ullrich. Do you have those sandwiches for me?"

"Right here." She fetches a brown paper bag from a shelf. "I added it to your tab."

"Thanks. Appreciate it." I toss a five-dollar bill into the tip jar and turn to leave. "Have a good day, ma'am."

"You, too, you handsome devil," she calls after me, making me grin.

I haven't exactly become a member of the community. I'm not one to attend town hall meetings and get acquainted with my neighbors.

But there's value in knowing who's here, who I should watch out for, and letting the community know that I'm not someone to be wary of.

I'm an outsider. I know that. But I keep to myself, and I don't make trouble. In return, the townspeople have been cordial, and I trust that I'm safe here.

Which is more important now than ever before.

When I walk out of the deli, I feel my blood fucking boil.

"In the car," I bark to Ivie, who's standing on the sidewalk, covered in puppies. "Now."

She smiles at the teenager who's walking them, gives one a kiss on the head, and then climbs in next to me.

"Don't yell at me, Shane. They're *puppies.*"

"I don't care if they were the cutest puppies on the planet—"

"Which they were."

"I told you to stay put. What if there had been a sniper in one of these buildings?"

She stares at me as I pull onto the road and head back toward home.

"You're being ridiculous."

"No, I'm not."

"There are no *snipers.*"

"That you know of."

"For God's sake, Shane, I was out of the car for less than fifteen seconds. I wanted to pet a puppy."

"Fifteen seconds is all they need. Trust me. We won't be leaving the ranch again."

"So now I'm being punished? I'm taking that blowjob back."

I want to laugh. But I'm too fucking mad.

CHAPTER 10

~IVIE~

"*I*'m going to—" Shane begins when we pull up to the house, but I put my hand up, stopping him from speaking further.

"I don't care what you're going to do. I'm not speaking to you right now."

I shove out of the SUV and hurry into the house. I hear him behind me, and I remember that I'm starving, so I whirl back and reach for the bag in his hands.

"Which one is mine?"

He doesn't reply, so I glance up at him and cock a brow.

"Shane?"

"Now you're speaking to me?"

I just narrow my eyes menacingly, and he's smart enough to sigh and hang his head. "They're the same."

I fetch one of the sandwiches from the bag and turn

to march away once more, headed for the guest room, where I shut and lock the door behind me.

I'm adult enough to restrain myself from *slamming* the door. Barely.

"He drives me fucking crazy," I mutter as I unwrap the sandwich and pull my phone out of my purse to video call my best friend, Annika. I've been friends with the gorgeous doctor for more years than I can count, and she knows *everything* there is to know about me.

She'll talk me down from the ledge.

"Hey, friend," she says with a bright smile. I prop the phone on the desk so I can see her, and vice versa, and still eat my lunch.

"I'm going to be eating in your ear."

"I'll join you. I just made some leftover lasagna for lunch."

"Lasagna leftovers are the *best*."

"Hell yes, they are," she agrees and takes a bite. "I'm so happy you called. I haven't heard from you since you went up to Shane's place."

"Oh, I'll likely get into trouble for this call, but I just don't give a shit. He made me mad, and I want to vent."

"Tell me everything." She wipes her mouth with a napkin. "And I do mean *everything.*"

"He's mad at me because I got out of the car when we went to the deli to pick up lunch."

"Why would he get mad?"

"He's totally overprotective," I say, getting riled up.

"I mean, I know he's just trying to protect me, but I was out of the car for less than a minute, petting puppies. *Puppies*, Annika. And he flew off the handle and said I could have been taken out by a sniper."

She frowns as she chews on some bread. "Do they have a lot of snipers in the mountains?"

"Right? That was my thought. I highly doubt it. But he was pissed off, and that made me mad. So, here we are. I told him I was taking the blowjob back."

Annika coughs and has to take a drink of her water. "Wait. What? *Blowjob*? Ivie Jordan, you're not telling me everything. Stop babbling about snipers and get to the good stuff. You know I'm living vicariously through you."

"You don't have to," I remind her. "Rafe—"

"We're not talking about Rafe. We're talking about you and blowjobs. Spill it. Right now."

"Oh, we're sleeping together."

I feel the smile spread slowly over my face.

"*Ivie.*"

"Okay, so you know we've been flirting for months and talking a ton. There's some serious attraction there. Not just on *my* part, which is still kind of a mystery to me. I mean, have you seen him? What does he see in me?"

"Ask me that again, and you'll no longer be my best friend." She narrows her eyes at me. "There are a million reasons to love you, and I'll send you an essay on the subject later. Tell me more."

"Well, the chemistry is off the charts. There has been sex. Like, really good sex. I finally know what all the fuss is about. I mean, I'm not a virgin, but I'm the girl boys had sex with on a dare or because they were drunk. And it's not like it was a fantastic time for me. But Shane takes his time and pretty much worships every inch of my body."

"You bitch."

I laugh, and Annika joins me.

"You know I love you and mean that in the nicest way possible."

"Of course." I take a bite and think about the frustrating man in question. "The Martinelli brothers are ridiculously sexy. Like, their gene pool must be made of gold."

"You're not kidding. Hotter than hot. And for a long time, my family didn't mesh well with theirs, but with Nadia and Carmine marrying soon, things have mellowed out. Which makes me happy."

"I like Carmine for Nadia."

Nadia is my other best friend. The three of us have been tight for a long time, and I'm so happy for her, that she found love with Carmine—even if he was the last person in the world anyone thought she'd end up with.

"But let's not talk about them. Let's talk about you," Annika suggests. "What else is going on? I miss you. I can't wait for this whole mess to be resolved so you can come home."

"Me, too." I sigh and roll my empty sandwich wrapper into a ball, tossing it into a nearby trash can. "It's really pretty up here, I have to admit. I can see why Shane likes it. But it's so far away from everything. So isolated."

"I assume that was the point of it," she says.

"A fortress in the mountains. Well, if that's what he was going for, that's what he got. The house is really nice. And he has a bunch of other buildings on the property. And a farmhand. Is that what it's called?"

Annika giggles. "Is the farmhand hot?"

"Actually, yeah. Kinda. He's the strong, silent type. Doesn't say much, but he's nice."

"Maybe I should make a trip to the ranch," Annika says, waggling her eyebrows.

"You have no idea how much I would *love* that."

"Ivie," Shane calls through the door. "Who are you talking to?"

I roll my eyes and move to the door, then unlock it to open it just a crack. "None of your business."

"Are you on your *cell phone*?" He stares at me like I've lost all my marbles.

"Of course, I am. I'm talking to Annika, and—"

"Not anymore, you're not. Sorry, Annika, I'm hanging up on you."

He ends the FaceTime call and rounds on me.

"I know you did *not* just hang up on my best friend."

"Why would you call her in the first place?"

"Because she's my best friend, and you're being a

dick, and I needed to vent about *you!*" I shout in his face. "That's what girls do, Shane. We vent when the guy we're sleeping with is being a douche canoe."

"You can't call out on your phone," he says and props his hands on his hips. "Anyone who's looking for you, who knows your number, can trace it here."

"You never told me that."

"You're a smart woman," he replies. "I would think you'd just know it."

I laugh and pace the room. "I'm not into espionage or finding people, Shane. How would I know that? It's something from movies."

"No, it's very real. This isn't a funny situation."

"You're right." I sober and face him. "There's nothing funny about it. Your behavior over the past hour has been disrespectful and just shitty all around."

"*My* behavior?" he demands. "Mine?"

"Yes, yours."

"Ivie, you were careless."

"How do you know?" I prop my hands on my hips. "You just made a split-second decision that I was being careless, but you didn't ask me anything. You assumed that I was stupid, and you punished me for it."

"Okay. Tell me what you were doing."

I just stare at him, still fuming.

"Please."

"The young boy who was walking those puppies fell. He was being pulled, and he wasn't strong enough to hold onto them. He fell right next to your car. I

117

surveyed the area, knew that I had my weapon on me, and decided to get out and help him right himself. It took ten seconds. Then you walked outside and threw a fit."

"I did not—"

"Oh, yes, you did. I'm not a child. I chose to help the boy after I weighed the situation. I didn't feel like I was in danger. Especially knowing that you'd return any second."

"I told you to stay in the car."

"And I'm sure you're used to people following your orders."

"To the letter," he agrees.

"I'm not your subordinate." I raise my chin. "You're teaching me to defend myself. I'm not an idiot, and I won't be treated like one."

"That's not—"

Before he can finish the sentence, a loud beeping starts, and he holds up his hand to shush me, then cocks his ear, listening.

"Fuck," he mutters and runs out of the room. I'm right on his heels as he opens the door of the 007 room downstairs as I've come to think of it, and we hurry down the stairs. He flicks a switch, and all of the monitors on one wall come to life.

"These are cameras showing the whole property," I mutter.

"Someone breached the perimeter," he says grimly and presses his phone to his ear. "Yeah, I hear it. I'm looking at the monitors, but I don't see anything. The alarm was tripped in quadrant forty-two. Okay. Yeah, I'll go check, too. You take the south and east sides, I'll take north and west, and we'll cover quadrants forty through forty-five. They can't have gotten far. Report back. Out."

He turns to me, his eyes flat and cold, and his voice is hard. "I need you to stay *here.* Do not go upstairs. Do not leave this room. I'll lock it on my way out. It's bomb-proof, fireproof, and impossible to get into if you don't know the code."

"Shane—"

"I don't know who's on my property, but they're about to get a rude awakening. Stay, Ivie. Keep your weapon on you, in case."

"I won't leave."

He nods once and starts to leave, but then he turns back to me and kisses me hard. He releases me as quickly as he grabbed me, takes the stairs two at a time, and then he's gone. The locks snick into place, and I'm left alone. To worry.

I turn back to the monitors. I see Shane exiting the back door, his weapon drawn as he takes off at a run.

Movement catches my eye on another monitor. It's Curt, also hurrying from his cabin, weapon drawn.

Jesus, it feels like something out of a mystery novel.

I wish I had sound.

I narrow my eyes as Curt and Shane come in and

out of range of the different cameras. Each monitor is labeled with a number.

"Shane said quadrant forty-two," I mutter, looking at the corresponding screen. I walk to it, looking for switches. "Nothing."

Curt and Shane continue coming and going, making their way through the thirties until they're in the quadrants in question.

I tap a couple of keys on a keyboard and pray with all my might that I don't fuck something up.

Suddenly, I can hear what's happening.

"Jackpot," I murmur, pleased that I haven't lost my touch when it comes to electronics.

"Nothing," I hear Curt say as he meets Shane in quadrant forty-four.

But then I see something in quadrant thirty-eight. I pick up the phone I grabbed on our way down here and text Shane.

Me: *Q38. Man with rifle.*

Shane looks at the smartwatch on his wrist, then crouches and gestures to Curt. I can't hear what he whispers to the other man, but they move fast and sleek from the monitor, through the others, making their way to the intruder.

"Oh, God," I whisper as I clasp my hands and press them to my chest. "Be careful. Who the hell is that?"

For two men crouched so low to the ground, they move fast. Suddenly, they're coming at the stranger from opposite sides.

"Stop right there," Shane commands, pointing his weapon at the man. "Drop the rifle."

"Hey," the guy says and raises his hands, slowly lowering his gun to the ground. "I'm not looking for any trouble."

"What *are* you looking for?" Shane asks as Curt retrieves the weapon and walks with it out of range of the stranger.

"Elk," the man says. "I'm just hunting elk."

"You're doing it on private property," Shane informs him. "*My* private property."

"I didn't realize I left state land."

"Bullshit," Curt mutters. "There are signs everywhere, asshole."

"Not to mention, I don't know of anyone around here who would shoot an elk with an assault weapon." Shane steps closer and pushes his pistol into the other man's face. "Who do you work for?"

"I'm just hunting elk." But the other man doesn't blink. Doesn't even look scared.

I'm terrified, and I'm safe in this room.

"Who sent you?" Curt asks and relieves the man of his wallet. "And is your last name really Sugarbaker?"

"Sugarbaker?" Shane smirks, but the man moves quickly, takes Shane's pistol, and rounds on Curt when he advances. There's a fight, a gunshot, and the camera goes dark.

"Oh, God." I tap keys frantically, but I can't get the feed or the sound back. They're just *gone.*

"No. Don't do this to me, Shane. Move into the range of another camera."

But they don't. In fact, systematically, every monitor goes dark.

Minutes that feel like hours tick by, but there's nothing.

Absolutely nothing.

Until the sound of another gunshot comes through another monitor. I don't see anything, but I hear the shot.

Jesus, is Shane hurt? Is Curt injured?

How can I be expected to just sit here and *wait*?

I try to call Shane's phone, but there's no reply.

"He told me to *stay*," I remind myself. "He'll be pissed if I don't."

I chew my lip.

"But he could be hurt. Oh, God, did more men show up? How long am I supposed to wait here? What if they're both bleeding out there somewhere?"

I can't just sit here on my hands. I *can't*.

I check my weapon and keep it in my hand as I climb the steps to the first floor. I put my hand on the knob and take a long, deep breath.

He's going to be *so mad*.

But I need to know that he's okay.

I bite my lip and turn the knob. When I open the door, I come face-to-face with Shane himself. He's bleeding. And he's *so pissed*.

"What in the fucking hell are you doing?"

CHAPTER 11

~IVIE~

"Oh, my God." I collapse against him and hold onto him. "Where are you bleeding? Who was that creep? What happened to him? Is Curt okay? I was worried sick, Shane. All the monitors went blank, and I didn't know if you were the one who got shot. I didn't know what to do. I couldn't just stay down there by myself; I was going crazy."

"You were supposed to stay put."

I lean back to look up at him, relieved when there's no fury in his gorgeous brown eyes. "But what if you were dying?"

"Then you still stay put. There's nothing you can do if that's the case." He wipes a tear I didn't even know was there from under my eye. He doesn't look nearly as mad as I expected him to be. "Come on."

"Where are we going?"

"My bedroom. I need to clean up, and we need to talk about you following orders."

I sigh, in both relief and defeat, but follow him down the hall to his bedroom and through to the bathroom. He strips out of his shirt, and I gasp at the hole in his arm.

"You were shot!"

"Yeah, it stings like a bitch. Just grazed me, but those hurt worse than the alternative, if you want to know the truth."

I just stand and stare at him. "Shane."

He glances up at me as he pulls supplies from a medicine cabinet.

"You were *shot.*"

"It's not the first time. Probably not the last. It's not too bad."

I shake my head and cross to him, pushing his hands aside as I begin to dress the wound. "Tell me everything."

"In a second. I don't want to fight about this anymore, Ivie. I'm not trying to control you or be a douche canoe, as you put it. I'm trying to keep you alive. And if you don't follow my orders to the letter, you put yourself at risk."

"I won't apologize for needing to know if you're dead or alive." I look him in the eyes and lean in to kiss his cheek. "I was so scared." My voice is a whisper. "I knew I'd be okay because you're here. And even if that asshole had killed you, you'd probably find a way to be a ghost and kick his ass if he tried to put his hands on me. You'll protect me no matter what, Shane. I needed to know if you were okay."

"I'm okay." He tips his forehead against mine. "I had a bad minute when he fought back. You said the screens went black?"

"Yeah, he must have shot the camera. They all went out. But not before I saw him struggle with you, take your gun, and then it went off. I was a mess of nerves."

"I was afraid that would happen to the monitors. The fucker who wired them did it wrong. I'll look at them."

"Forget the monitors. How was he able to surprise you like that?"

"We were laughing at his last name. I didn't expect him to fight back, honestly. And that's my fault. I know better than to let my guard down for even a second. We recovered quickly, but the damage was done. It was a stupid mistake, and one I don't plan to repeat."

"Is Curt okay?"

"Yes."

"Is the other guy dead?"

Shane's eyes are calm. And cold. "Yes."

I swallow hard and resume dressing his wound, keeping my fingers gentle. "Did you kill him?"

He takes my hand and kisses my knuckles. "I didn't have to."

"Curt killed him?"

"He self-terminated," he replies. "I don't know who

he was. Curt's running him right now. We found his vehicle on the road where he breached the property. Got a name and some info on him, but I've never heard of him before."

"He was here for me."

Shane's hand tightens on mine. "He never admitted to that, but I'm pretty sure he was. He could have been sent in to assassinate me. We'll know after Curt gets more info."

"You?" I scowl at him. "Why would anyone want to kill you?"

There's no humor in his laugh. "I've committed dozens, if not hundreds of sins in my lifetime, Ivie."

"We all have."

He cups my face gently. "Not like me. I belong to a very small club, honey."

"So, you're never safe."

"I wouldn't say that."

"I wish you'd tell me more. Help me understand you. I just want to know you, Shane."

"You do know me. In all the ways that matter. Now, get this sewn up before I bleed out."

"I don't think you're going to bleed out. You don't even need stitches." But I reach for the antiseptic and dab at the wound. "You took his gun away. How did he kill himself?"

"He had a blade. Cut his own throat."

I still and stare down at him with my mouth agape. "Jesus."

"That's what I thought."

"What did you do with his body?"

He kisses the inside of my wrist. "It won't be found. Well, animals might get him, but that's it. The body, and the vehicle, are long gone."

"So, I shouldn't ask questions."

"You can ask them. I don't know how much I'll tell you, though. The less you know, the better."

I don't necessarily agree with that, but I keep my opinion to myself and cover the injury. After I put the supplies away, I turn to walk out of the bathroom, but Shane snags my wrist and tugs me back into his arms.

"I'm sorry I was gruff with you," he says against my hair. I melt against him, soaking in his warmth and strength. "I need to keep you safe. Not because you're a job to me, Ivie. But because if anything were to ever happen to you, I don't think I would survive it."

My heart might explode from the admission. I glance up at him, but before I can say anything, Shane crushes his mouth to mine and lifts me, carrying me to the bed.

"The thought of you being hurt out there was pure torture," I admit against his lips as he tugs my shirt out of my jeans. "I know I should have stayed. But I couldn't *see* you. I heard the gunshot, and I didn't know. Shane—"

"I know." He gently covers my mouth with his. "I know, baby."

The room is hushed and dim with the blinds closed

as, without a word, we undress and come together once more. Our touches are just a little more reverent. Our kisses linger, and each breath, each moment is more beautiful than the last.

We tumble over the linens, and when we join, I gasp and then moan as he begins to move, thrusting in just the right rhythm to make my body sing in pleasure.

His fingers lace with mine, and he pins my hands above my head.

"You're gorgeous," he mutters before nibbling on my lips. "You're *everything.*"

I tilt my hips, meeting every thrust, then tighten around him as the orgasm moves through me, taking me by surprise.

"That's it," he whispers. "Let go, baby."

"Shane."

His body clenches above mine, and his hands tighten on mine as he lets himself go.

And later, when we're lying together in the waning light of the afternoon, he turns to me for more.

"Brutus Sugarbaker," Curt says with a shrug. We're all sitting in the 007 room, eating pizza and staring at the monitor. Brutus's face fills the screen. It looks like a mugshot. "Forty-seven. From Atlanta."

"What was he doing in the middle of Colorado?" Shane wants to know.

"Not hunting elk," I murmur and take a bite of pepperoni. "He wasn't dressed like a hunter. If he was trying to blend in as someone from here, a hunter, he didn't do a good job of it."

"Hardly," Curt agrees. "However, I did a *lot* of digging, and I can't trace him back to any syndicate. He doesn't work for the government. He doesn't seem to belong to anyone. He was born and raised in Georgia, not far from Atlanta."

"Family?" I ask.

"A wife and three kids." I frown, but Curt keeps talking. "On the surface. It's a cover. I dug a little deeper. His name is Art Fink. How he came up with Sugarbaker, I don't know."

"*Designing Women*, of course." Both men turn and stare at me. "The TV show from the eighties. Come on, surely you've heard of it. I mean, I was hardly *born* in the eighties, but even I know about it. It's a classic."

"Nope," Curt says, but I do get a half-smile out of him, and I consider that a win. "However, just because I uncovered his legal name, doesn't mean I found much of anything else. No marriage on file. No kids. Also, like Brutus Sugarbaker, no ties to any organization. Just the vehicle registration, the one he had with him. No mortgage. No credit history."

"How can he have no credit history?" I demand. "Surely, he can't be a ghost. Is this another false name?"

"I found the birth certificate," Curt replies.

"Did you find what he does for a living?" Shane asks.

"No."

Shane blows out a breath. "So, we still don't know who, exactly, he was trying to find. He could have been here for Ivie or me."

"Or me, really," Curt says philosophically. "God knows I've pissed people off over the years."

"No way," I say, shaking my head. "You're too sweet and quiet."

"Keep flirting with Curt, and I'll break his legs," Shane snarls.

Now Curt does smile, showing off straight, white teeth. "Fooled you, have I?"

"No." I shake my head and reach for another slice of the delicious pizza. "I know shitty people when I see them. Trust me, I've seen my fair share, especially when I was younger. I've seen the worst of the worst. The scariest. You're not that, Curt."

"Hmm," is all he says in reply. "Well, whoever this Fink asshole was, he won't be bothering us again. What I want to know is, who sent him, and who was he supposed to report back to?"

"The million-dollar question," Shane agrees. "He worked for someone, and they'll be looking for him. Did you find anything on his phone?"

"Nope. He had no email loaded on it, no text messages. It was wiped clean. No calls, in or out."

"On the *phone*," I say, thinking it over.

"That's right."

"But not on the number itself. Gimme." I motion for Curt to hand over the cell, which he does. I open it and frown when I see it's locked.

"I have the—" Curt begins, but I cut him off with a sharp shake of my head and tap the screen.

"These are easy to break open," I say and smile when the screen opens. "Ah, you're right. It looks like it's straight from the factory. No apps, no messages. No call log. However, I can get the number off of it and do a little hacking on the computer."

I find the phone number and sit at the computer. I crack my knuckles, shift my head back and forth, and then get down to business. My fingers fly across the keyboard as I search the number, find the carrier, and hack into their system.

"Jesus," Curt mutters in surprise. "You're in their server."

"Yeah, we're going to find out who this jerk talked to. This is a burner phone, but I can still find out what calls came in and out, and we can search those numbers, trace them back to their owners. He wasn't speaking to everyone on burner phones. That's impossible. And it's a mistake that's going to help us."

I type furiously, excited at the idea of helping, of getting to the bottom of this.

"I know solving this won't solve *everything*, but it's a start. Okay, he called four people. Write these numbers down."

Shane pulls out a notepad and pen and scribbles furiously.

"How am I supposed to read this?" I demand when I glance down. "Are you sure you're not a doctor with that chicken scratch?"

"Who owns the numbers?" he asks.

"Okay, this first one is owned by an Oliver Freemont. Lives in New York."

"Got it," Shane says, still scribbling. "No idea who that is. The next?"

"Give me a second." This one doesn't want to give so easily. "It could be another burner phone. It's under some layers, which is unusual. I've got it. Billy Sergi."

"What?" Shane demands. "Look again."

"It's registered to a Billy Sergi."

"Motherfucker son of a bitch."

"Who's Billy Sergi?" I ask in confusion, but Shane shakes his head.

"Who else, Ivie?" he asks.

I move on to the third number. "This one *is* a burner phone. No specific owner. Working on the fourth now."

I keep typing. When I sit back, I stare at the monitor in disbelief.

"Well?" Shane demands.

"There's no possible way, Shane. It has to be a mistake."

"Who is it registered to?"

I turn my gaze up to his and shake my head. I don't believe it. I *can't* believe it.

Rather than ask me again, Shane leans over to look over my shoulder. When he sees the name on the screen, he swears under his breath.

"That's impossible."

I stand and pace the room. "Well, I guess we know who he was here to find."

"There's a mistake," Shane insists and starts typing on another screen. "This is a cover for someone else, to throw us for a loop."

Well, if that's what someone's trying to do, it's working. Because my head is spinning. I can't breathe.

"Hey," Curt says and taps Shane on the shoulder. "Your girl's panicking."

"How can this be?" I wonder aloud and continue pacing the room until I run into a brick wall of a chest. Shane's arms close around me in comfort. "He's dead."

"It's meant to fuck with you," Shane assures me. "And you're letting it."

I pull back to stare up at him. "Wouldn't you?"

"It would throw me, yes. But keep your wits about you, sweetheart. This isn't real. It's smoke and mirrors. And if the person I think is behind this is truly responsible, it fits his M.O. perfectly."

"Who?"

"Sergi," he says simply. "And if he's responsible, I'm going to be fucking pissed off."

I pull out of Shane's arms and return to the computer.

"I'm going to keep digging because there has to be a mistake," I say as my fingers start to fly over the keyboard once more. But no matter where I dig, no matter where I look, I keep getting the same result.

And I can't accept that.

Because the owner that keeps popping up on the screen is my father, and he's been dead for more than a decade.

CHAPTER 12

~SHANE~

*J*vie's skin is soft where I kiss her, right next to her eyebrow, and then I silently back out of the room. She's sleeping peacefully, which is exactly what she needs after the mind fuck that she went through in my office.

I close the door behind me and walk out to the living room, where Curt sits, waiting for me.

"She's finally asleep." I pour myself two fingers of whiskey and do the same for Curt. After passing him the glass, I collapse into my favorite leather chair. "This whole thing is fucking nuts."

"I've seen some shit, you know I have." Curt sips his whiskey. "But I don't know if I've ever seen anything like this before."

"Yeah, it's not typical, that's for sure."

I stare at my friend, lost in thought. I saw all of

what Curt did—and plenty more since. Curt was on my squad. Was the best assassin I've ever worked with.

He's quick, stealthy, and ruthless. When he needed to leave, to disappear, I knew I had to have him here on the ranch. I'd trust no one more to make sure things run smoothly here when I'm gone.

And I'm gone plenty.

"You know you should leave," he says, surprising me.

"I live here."

He shakes his head and then pins me with that intense stare he gets when he knows things are about to go to hell.

"Take her out of here. If that idiot found her, it's only a matter of time before someone else does."

I blow out a breath and then take another sip of whiskey. "Even if they do find her, I can protect her here better than anywhere else. I know every inch of this land like the back of my hand. And so do you. We can take on an army here if we need to."

"I think it's the wrong move, but you're the boss."

"We keep our eyes open and remain on high alert for the foreseeable future." I lean forward, my elbows resting on my knees, and stare into my glass. "I know that this isn't what you signed on for, man. If you want to go somewhere and lay low until this all blows over, I won't be angry or think any differently of you."

He swallows the rest of his whiskey and sets the glass down without a sound. "I'm not afraid. What happened today didn't give me any bad moments. I thought it might, but I slipped back into the job, you know?"

"Yeah." I nod once. "I know."

"But I came here so I wouldn't have to do that anymore. I know you think it was cowardly of me—"

"Hold up." I raise a hand and scowl at my friend. "You're no coward. You did what you had to do to survive, Curt. You did more on the job than anyone else has. It was too big an ask, and it was wrong."

"It was the motherfucking *job*," he insists. "And it sucked, but it was just the job. And maybe because of that, I can't do it anymore. But I won't leave this land. I won't run away and hide. If they're brave enough to come here and fuck with us, we'll show them just how stupid they are."

I nod grimly. "Damn right. But this isn't your fight."

"It's yours, and that makes it mine."

He says it so simply. As if there's no other way of doing things. As if it's as easy as breathing.

"You'd do the same for me," he continues.

"Without hesitation."

His lips twitch.

"So, you're not leaving, then?"

"Not yet." I shake my head and rub my hand over my lips in agitation. "But I need to call my brothers and Cox. I need to know what the fuck is going on. If that piece of shit Billy Sergi is behind this, I'll kill him myself."

"And start a war in the process," Curt adds, knowing very well that the Sergi family is a force to be reckoned with. The mafia family is based in New York, and our families don't always see eye-to-eye.

I wouldn't put this past them.

"If they're trying to kill Ivie, it won't be a war. I'll end them."

Curt stares at me for a moment and then mutters, "*Fuck,*" under his breath before scrubbing his hands over his face.

"Sure you don't want to go lay low somewhere for a while?" I ask.

There's no humor in his laugh. "Oh yeah, I do. But I won't. We'll finish this. I'm going to go secure that fence line and make sure the alarms are set. I don't want any more surprises."

"Great. I'm going to make some calls. I'll be sticking close to the house while Ivie sleeps."

He nods and stands, but then turns back to me. "You're in love with her."

It's not a question.

"I know that it can't go anywhere." I sigh again. "But, yeah. She's incredible."

"Does she know? What you do?"

"No. And she won't."

"Shane—"

"The less she knows, the better."

"I'm just going to say this, as your friend. She's a smart girl. She's not weak. And she deserves to know the truth so she can make the decision for herself. It's not your place to decide for her."

"I'm protecting her."

"Did she ask you to?" He raises a brow, and with that, he walks out of the house.

It's damn annoying to have people in my life who are so fucking smart—and stick their noses into my business.

I reach for my phone and start with Cox.

"Yeah, yeah, I'm working on it," he says by way of greeting.

"Work faster," I suggest and fill him in on what happened today.

"If I move any faster, I'll raise flags, and people will start asking questions," he says, frustration heavy in his voice. "Jesus, Shane, what did this girl do?"

"Nothing. That's just it. This is all about her father. And it's pissing me the fuck off."

"Yeah, well, I'm moving as fast as I can without putting everyone at risk, but I should hear back from the one contact I've reached out to tomorrow morning."

"Meet me in Denver at noon tomorrow."

He blows out a breath. "No pressure or anything."

"Oh, there's plenty of fucking pressure. I'm going to call my brothers and ask them to meet us there because this goes deeper than I thought. I don't want to talk about it over the phone."

"Yeah, okay. I'll see you tomorrow. You're annoying, you know that?"

I grin. "Yeah. I know. Thanks for noticing."

I hang up and immediately dial Carmine's number.

"Yo," he says, his usual greeting. He only does it with Rocco and me because it always made us laugh as kids.

Old habits die hard.

"I need you guys closer," I say and explain again what happened today. "I have details that I can't talk about on the phone. Cox is meeting me in Denver at noon."

"We'll head that way tonight. Nadia wants to do some shopping for the wedding anyway."

"I'm so glad I could accommodate your fiancée's shopping needs."

"I heard that," Nadia says into my ear. "And thanks. I can kick ass *and* shop."

"Who says I need you to help me kick ass?"

She laughs. "You three wouldn't know how to kick ass without me, Shane."

"We did just fine for a long time without you," I remind her.

"Okay, kids," Carmine interrupts. "We'll see you tomorrow. Noon."

He clicks off, and I feel marginally better after some light verbal sparring with Nadia and knowing that I'll have my brothers nearby in just a few hours.

I know that I *can* do this without them. But I don't have to. And that feels damn good.

"Hey."

My head whips up at the sound of Ivie's voice. She's standing at the edge of the room, her hair tousled from sleep. She's chewing her lip as if she's not sure what to do.

"Come here." I hold out my hand for her, and when she crosses to me, I tug her into my lap where I can cuddle her. "How do you feel?"

"Drowsy. I woke up and didn't know what year it was." She smiles softly. "But it was also refreshing."

"Good. You needed it."

She plays with the button on my Henley and rests her cheek on my shoulder. "What have you been up to?"

"Making calls, talking with Curt. The usual."

"I don't think today was *usual*."

"No, you're right. It wasn't. I can honestly say that I haven't had any excitement out here since I built the ranch."

"And yet, it's built to be a fortress."

"Came in handy today." I kiss her forehead. I can't keep my lips or my hands to myself. She's a fucking siren.

"So, what's the latest?"

I don't want to give her too much information because I want to *protect* her, but then Curt's words come back to my mind, and I decide to take them to heart.

Because he's right. She's intelligent and capable.

141

And maybe I'm doing her a disservice by keeping the details from her.

At least where this current situation is concerned.

"I'm headed into Denver tomorrow morning," I begin and tell her about meeting with Cameron and my family. "We're going to come up with more answers and a plan for moving forward."

"What time do we leave?" she asks.

"*We* aren't going. I am."

Ivie scowls. "You're killing me here, Shane. I *need* to go with you, for my mental health."

"And I *need* you to stay here, for your physical safety. I won't risk taking you into the city. You'll stay here with Curt."

"Great, so I have a babysitter." She pouts, and I can't resist taking her mouth with mine, nibbling that plump lower lip.

"He's not a babysitter. He's a companion. Don't flirt with him."

She grins at that, which was exactly my intention. "I could use that time to try to get more information out of him. I'm determined to be his friend."

"Good luck with that. I'll be back tomorrow afternoon. It'll be a quick trip."

"Okay." She sighs. "This all sucks balls."

I can't help myself. I wrap my arms around her and hold her tightly against me. "Yeah, it does."

"I mean, I thought I'd get to spend time with you

and get to know you better under much different circumstances. I didn't think we'd be forced into it."

I scowl. "I don't think that we're being *forced* into anything."

"Aren't we? I'm not allowed to leave. You have to stay here to protect me. Feels pretty forced. And I'm not complaining, I'm just saying it's not a fun way to start seeing a guy. Pretty unconventional, actually."

"Well, I never was the traditional type, I guess."

She laughs and then sighs. "So, what do you want to do this evening?"

I raise a brow, thinking it over. "You seem to be feeling better."

"I'm just fine, thank you for asking."

I stand with her still in my arms and walk through the living room, down the hall to my bedroom.

"Do you want to take another nap?" I love this playful side of her.

"That's not what I had in mind, actually." I set her gently on the bed and climb on next to her, my head braced in my hand and the other one gliding down her torso. She's wearing an orange tank and black shorts.

No bra, as evidenced by her tightening nipples.

"Do you want to talk some more?" she asks, all innocence.

"Yeah, I want to talk."

She glances up in surprise. "Okay, what do you want to talk about?"

"How fucking sexy you are," I reply as my hand glides up her smooth stomach, under the tank top that was clearly designed to drive a man out of his fucking mind.

"That's not a fun conversation."

"I think you're wrong." I scoot down to kiss the skin I just uncovered. "I think it's the best conversation ever. And it's going to take us a while to go through all of the talking points."

"Did you make a PowerPoint presentation?"

I chuckle as I unearth one perfect breast. "I should. Maybe I will, actually. I'll have to include photos. So, I should probably take some pictures of your perfect body."

"A: My body isn't perfect by any stretch of the imagination. And B: No one, and I do mean *no one,* will ever take naked photos of me. It would ruin my political career."

I snort and then look at her in surprise. "You want to be a politician?"

"Of course, not. But if I did, it would ruin it. So, no photos."

"I guess that means I'll just have to commit everything to memory." I pluck the nipple with my lips, enjoying the way her back arches at my touch. "Like that?"

"Yeah. I like that."

"There's much more where that came from."

"Are you going to tell me or show me?"

"Both." I surprise her by flipping her over onto her

belly and then cup her round ass in my hands. "You have a stellar ass, Ivie. You've just gotta love any god you pray to for making an ass like this."

"You're crazy." She giggles and then sighs when I slip my fingers up the hem of the leg of her shorts and graze her most intimate lips. "How do you do this to me when I'm still fully clothed?"

"Talent." I kiss the small of her back. "I don't mean to brag, but I'm a dedicated worker. I take my job of making you feel fucking amazing very seriously."

"Holy shit, Shane."

"What's up, Ivie?" I can't help but grin when she pushes that ass off the bed in the best fucking invitation I've ever had.

"Oh my God." Her hands fist in the bedsheets, and I know she's close. I haven't even pushed a finger inside her yet. I've only teased.

Her responsiveness is the most arousing thing I've ever seen in my life. I can't get enough of her. I want to explore her, to just submerge myself in her for about a year.

And it still wouldn't be enough.

"You're almost there," I murmur and kiss up her spine as my fingers continue playing her like an instrument.

There are no more words coming out of her now. No, it's just moans and gasps, and when I finally slide a finger through the wetness and inside of her, she bucks and then falls apart.

When she's finished quaking, I turn her to face me and kiss the hell out of her.

"Small talk is over," I inform her with a grin and pull my shirt over my head. "Let's get to the good stuff."

"Oh. Right. Okay." She licks her lips. "Let's get to the good stuff."

CHAPTER 13

~IVIE~

"*Y*ou *have* to talk to me," I inform Curt as we sit in the barn, out of breath from sparring.

Shane being gone doesn't mean I get to be lazy. No, Curt informed me right away that we'd be working out most of the morning, which I don't mind. It keeps my mind occupied and off the scarier things.

Like men trying to kill me.

"About what?" he asks and takes a sip of water.

"Everything. I don't know anything about you, and I've been beating you up for *days*."

"I don't think you've beaten me up," he says with a frown. "I've let you get some punches in. To teach you."

"Right." I smirk and take a sip of water and then square my shoulders, determined to crack through his hard shell. "Let me just ask ten questions."

"That's a lot of questions," he says. "A lot."

"I have a hundred, so it's not really that much. Deal?"

He sighs and stares at me with guarded eyes. "I reserve the right to say, '*no comment*.'"

"Of course, I'm not a monster." I toss a sweatshirt over my shoulders to keep from getting chilled. "Okay, first question. What's your favorite meal to eat for dinner?"

He blinks, surprised. I want to laugh, but I don't. Does he think I'm going to start with the hard questions first? This isn't my first rodeo.

"Spaghetti, I guess. Because it's easy to make. I heat up a jar of sauce and cook some noodles."

I scrunch up my nose. "Ew. If that's your favorite, I will blow your mind with my spaghetti. I'll make it this week. Okay, question two. How old are you?"

"Thirty-four."

"Wow, you don't look thirty-four. I would have said late twenties."

"I feel eighty," he mutters, only intensifying my curiosity.

"What's your dream car?"

He grins, a full-on grin, and I'm struck by how handsome he is. I mean, he's not hotter than Shane, but he's a good-looking guy.

"1964 ½ Mustang convertible in cherry red."

I blink at him. "That's pretty specific. And...*old*."

"They're harder to find than they used to be, but it's a honey of a car. Purrs like a kitten."

"I'm going to take your word for it. I was never really a car person. I don't like to drive."

He frowns over at me. "You don't like to drive? Why not?"

"Well, because I'm super clumsy for one. I trip over my own feet. I warned Shane that I wouldn't be good with a loaded weapon or with sparring because I'd end up killing someone."

"You just need some confidence," Curt insists, and it makes me smile because it's exactly what Shane said. "When you have the confidence in your weapon, and it's an extension of *you*, you won't be clumsy with it."

"I'm getting better," I admit with a nod, wanting to keep the conversation moving. This is the most I've heard Curt speak since I got here. "But driving unnerves me because what if I don't see something that I should, or...I don't know? Anything could happen. I don't want to hurt anyone. I have a car, but I only drive to work and back home. That's really it."

"At least in Denver, there's a public transpo system."

"Exactly." I smile at him. "Are you originally from the city?"

"No. Small town in North Carolina, near the ocean."

"Oh, nice. I haven't been to either of the Carolinas, but I hear they're beautiful."

"Yeah, it's pretty nice over there."

I nod. "Is your family still there?"

"Some of them, yeah."

"Cool. That's something I always missed, you know? I just had my dad when I was little, and he was no prize, as you know. No siblings or extended family to speak of, at least in the US. I don't know if there was or is family in Bulgaria. He never spoke of it. So, I always felt like I didn't have roots."

"You've set down roots in Denver," he points out. "You have Annika and Nadia and their family."

"That's true." I smile as I think about it. "You're right. I guess family doesn't always mean being tied by blood."

"No, it doesn't."

"What did you do before you came to the ranch?"

He clams up now and shakes his head. "I think we should get over to the shooting range for some practice."

"You said I could ask ten questions. That was only, like, six."

He pushes his hand through his hair in agitation. "I worked with Shane in the military."

"Oh, wow. Thank you for your service."

He just gives me a stiff nod, and I decide to change course. "Do you have a girlfriend?"

"No." He snorts and shakes his head, his shoulders loosen. "Do you see any women out here? Besides you?"

"I'm sure there are single girls in town somewhere.

Or maybe a long-distance relationship. There are options."

"I'm kind of a loner, Ivie."

"Yeah, Shane mentioned that. Why is that?"

"Because I'm an introvert." He swallows hard. "And I'm not good with people."

"Well, I think you're just fine. But I get it. People can suck. You should see some of the patients that come into our clinic. Annika and I run a medi-spa. She's the doctor, and I'm the office manager. There are days that my eyes hurt from all the eye-rolls behind patients' backs."

His lips twitch. "Do you guys do nose jobs and stuff?"

"She can, but mostly we do botox, fillers, peels, that sort of thing. Annika is an amazing doctor. I think she should work in a reconstructive surgery practice. Help women who have lost their breasts to cancer or burn victims. She's really good. But her family was old-fashioned and didn't think she should do that."

"So, they're misogynistic, then."

I blink rapidly, thinking it over. "I guess so, actually. Her father and her uncle love her to distraction, but she's in a mafia family, and what they say goes. Not to mention, she's sometimes on call to help them out when someone's been hurt, and they don't want to involve a hospital."

Curt nods. "Yeah, the Martinellis have that, too. It's an…interesting way of life."

"I hate it," I admit. "And I'm on the outside, looking in. Even though Annika's family treats me like I'm one of theirs, I don't have the same responsibilities that she does because I'm *not* blood. And I'm relieved. I had to do a lot for my father when I was young that no person should have to do. He wasn't technically part of any mafia organization, but he was dangerous and mean. And I always swore that I'd never get involved with anyone like that again."

"What happened?"

I glance at him, suddenly wondering how we turned the tables to questions about *me.*

"I met Annika in college. We didn't know anything about each other at all. But one night, we got drunk in our dorm room. And Annika started telling me about how her uncle was a boss and detailing the whole damn family tree. I was so surprised because she is just a normal girl, with an abnormal family. So, I felt comfortable telling her about me. And when we were done and had sobered up a bit, we knew that we would be friends for life. Because of shared experiences, and because we can trust each other."

"Honestly, that's very similar to my friendship with Shane," Curt says, surprising me. "We have shared experiences that most don't have. The trust is rock solid, and I would do anything for him."

I smile over at him. "See, this isn't hard."

"What?"

"Talking."

"I'm not used to it. It's outside my comfort zone."

"Usually, the best things in life are those outside our comfort zones."

Curt smirks and then glances down at his buzzing phone. "That's Shane. He's on his way back. Should be here in a couple of hours, at the most."

"Cool. Okay, let's go shoot some targets. I'm going to pretend they're that asshole from yesterday and teach him a lesson."

"You're a little scary sometimes. You know that, right?"

"Me?" I laugh as we lock up the barn and get in the ATV to drive over to the shooting range. "Nah. I'm a pussy cat. But that guy pissed me off. He could have hurt one of you. Or killed you."

"He didn't." Curt parks in front of the door in the side of the mountain, and we jump out. He places his hand on the palm plate, and once we're inside, he locks us in as I open the vault.

"I want to use something bigger today."

Curt arches a brow. "Feeling brave, are you?"

"I've been using this small 9mm. Shane upgraded me to it a few days ago. And I'm sure it's appropriate for me, but I want to try something a little...beefier."

"The sidearm that Shane assigned to you *is* perfect for you, and I'll tell you why. It's slim and perfect for the size of your hands. It's easy for you to manipulated and control. But it's a 9mm so the bullets are lethal. You have a lot of power in that weapon. If you start shooting something bigger, you run the risk of hurting yourself because it'll be more difficult to handle. And if you were ever confronted, it could be easier for the assailant to get it away from you.

"So, this is what you should master. Personally, I think you should carry two of them. One at the small of your back, and a clutch piece on your ankle."

"Wow. You really know this stuff."

"It was my job for a long time. And, no, I'm not going to talk about it."

"Killjoy."

He laughs at that and hangs a target for me, then sends it down the lane.

"Okay, using the weapon assigned to you, let's see what you've got."

"I CAN ADMIT when I'm wrong," I say as I finish reloading my weapon and tuck it into the small of my back. "You're right, this is the right size for me."

"It's good that we had you try a couple of others. You never know when you might have to pick up a discarded weapon and use it."

"I don't plan to go to war."

"No one does." He smiles thinly. "You'll be prepared for anything. That's not a bad thing."

"No, I suppose not."

We've just started to shut down the range when sirens start.

"Fuck," Curt says sharply and opens his phone. "We've been breached again."

"Oh, my God. Maybe it's Shane."

"Not Shane." His face is grim as he looks up at me. "There are several men, all in military gear. I'm not going to lie to you, Ivie. This isn't good. I want you to go through that door and take the tunnel to the bunker."

"I can help you."

"No." He shakes his head in frustration as he hurries back into the vault. I'm on his heels as he takes weapons out of cases, loads them, and stuffs his pockets with ammo. He tucks a knife into his pants, a small pistol at his ankle. He looks like Rambo. "You absolutely cannot. You're trained to protect yourself, not infiltrate. So, listen to me very carefully. You take that tunnel to the bunker, and you sit tight. You do *not* come out until someone comes for you."

"But—"

He's looking down at his phone as he types furiously. "I've just alerted Shane. I hope he's not out there in this mess. I mean it, Ivie. Stay in the bunker until someone comes to you. If it's a bad guy, you shoot them. Do you understand? Don't hesitate."

"I won't." I hurry to him and hug him hard. Curt stiffens. "Be smart out there."

"Get to the bunker," he says again, and then he's

gone. The door locks behind him, and I take a second to breathe long and deep.

Curt's out there, but he's armed to the gills.

I have two sidearms on me, and I open the vault to get more ammo, lock it behind me, and then do as I'm told and hurry through the tunnel.

Shane was smart enough to show me a map of the tunnel system down here and insisted I study it.

I'm so glad he did because it's not just one tunnel. I remember him telling me that there are tunnels to the main house, Curt's cabin, and the barn.

But I stay to the right, remembering the map, and am suddenly at a door. I open it, lights automatically come on, and I'm in the bunker.

I lock the door behind me and check the locks to the outside, and then I immediately look around for monitors.

Shane wouldn't hole up down here without being able to see what's happening above. I find a bathroom, the two bedrooms, and then stare at a small door that looks like it goes to a tiny closet.

"You disguised it." My heart is hammering when I open the narrow door and grin. I flip the lights on and sigh in relief.

It's a smaller version of the 007 room. I flip on computers and monitors and sigh in relief when the same cameras come to life.

"Oh, fuck." I lean in, watching in horror as at least a dozen men walk through the property, all on different monitors. "They've spread out. My God, it looks like an army."

It's not. A dozen men do not make an army, but it looks damn scary to me.

"There's Curt." I cover my mouth with my hand and watch as Curt sneaks up behind a man dressed in all black. With the swipe of an arm, he cuts the man's throat wide-open as if he's cutting through warm butter. I gasp and watch as the dead man falls at Curt's feet, and then Curt narrows his eyes and looks to his right.

Another man with an automatic weapon makes his way toward Curt, but Curt's too fast. He raises his hand and throws the knife, hitting the man square in the forehead.

"Christ." I have to turn away, unable to watch it. Curt's a trained killer. It's obvious in every move he makes that this is what he was taught to do. I don't know how to reconcile the man I was chatting with in the barn with this assassin.

I check the time. Shane should be back anytime. I hope Curt's message reached him, and he doesn't walk into this without being warned.

My God, they could kill him.

And it would all be my fault.

Why did he bring me here? Why did he put himself and Curt at risk?

Sure, we flirted a lot over the past few months, but it's not like he *owes* me anything. And now his property and his friend are at risk.

He is at risk.

Because of me.

If something happens to him, I'll never forgive myself.

CHAPTER 14

~SHANE~

"It's a party," Cameron says when my brothers and Nadia file into the office in downtown Denver. "I should have brought chips or something."

"Good to see you," Carmine says, shaking his hand.

"I wish it were under better circumstances," Cameron replies. When we're all seated around the room, me behind the desk, Rocco standing to my left, and Nadia and Carmine on the couch, Cameron gives his report.

"As far as I can tell, the Sergis were behind yesterday's attempt at a raid," Cameron says, making Carmine swear ripely. "I was able to do some digging and found ten-thousand dollars deposited into the asshole's account. I suspect it was just a scouting mission. If they were serious about getting in and grabbing Ivie, there would have been more than just one guy there."

"I thought the same," I add with a nod. "Why would Billy start a war with the Tarenkovs?"

"Because he's a piece of shit," Nadia says coldly. "He has to know that Ivie is one of ours. He's not stupid, and he was at Annika's wedding earlier this year. Not to mention, he has a grudge against me."

"The Sergis love money," Rocco adds.

"They have plenty of fucking money," I remind him.

"Come on, man," Rocco says. "You know he heard that there was a bounty on Ivie's head, dead or alive, and figured he'd cash in on the payday."

"A million dollars," I mutter, shaking my head. "He's willing to start a war over a measly million dollars. They're worth a hundred times that much."

"Billy's not particularly smart," Carmine adds. "I wonder if his father knows what his son's up to."

"I'm going to kill him."

All of the eyes in the room fly to me. Cameron scowls. "Shane—"

"I'm going to tie him up and disembowel him. Slowly. The son of a bitch will pay for this."

"There's more." Cameron stands to pace the office. "You said that Ivie kept coming up with her father's name as one of the owners of the phone numbers yesterday."

"What?" Carmine demands. "I thought he was long dead."

"We all did," I confirm, and can see from the look on Cameron's face that the man is very much alive.

"It was a cover," Cam says and blows out a breath. "If anyone finds out that I came into this information, my family and those closest to me could be at risk. The O'Callaghans can't be touched for this."

"They'll be protected," I assure him. "You all will."

"I'm trying to get the fuck out of this life," Cox reminds me and then shakes his head in disgust. "Okay, so about a dozen years ago, maybe a little more, a lot of people wanted Pavlov dead. He was a piece of shit, a bad businessman, and liked to borrow money that he never repaid. We won't even get into his lack of parenting skills.

"Anyway, I was part of a taskforce back then that was trying to find his whereabouts so we could get in, assassinate him, and get out."

"The government wanted him gone?" Rocco asks, surprised.

"Oh, yeah. He was a Bulgarian operative. It's all just a mess, and the world was better off without him. Anyway, before my team could get in and take care of him, someone supposedly beat us to it. Killed him. We saw a video of it, for fuck's sake. They hung him.

"We closed the case and forgot about it. Wrote it off. We had other missions to worry about, and while Pavlov was a pain in the ass, he was small potatoes compared to some of the things we do."

"But?" I ask.

"I made some calls, started asking around. Discretely. Called in some favors. It was a cover. Pavlov wasn't hanged that day. It was a guy who looked a lot like him. Turns out, Pavlov has been living in Dallas for at least a decade, still doing his shady shit but on a smaller scale."

"Who was behind this?" I demand, seeing red.

"Sergi." Cameron blows out a breath. "Pavlov was working on his turf. But Sergi didn't want him dead because Pavlov knew too many people, kept too many secrets. He needed him alive, just in case. So, he staged the murder, hid Pavlov away, and no one was the wiser.

"But, about a year ago, Pavlov fucked up again and pissed off some people. The wrong people. In Dallas. Who is the Dallas syndicate?"

"It used to be the Carlitos," Carmine says thoughtfully. "But the boss died twenty years ago, and no one was interested in taking over."

"Apparently, that changed, too," Cox replies. "A kid by the name of Benji Carlito has decided to take up the reins. He's twenty-four."

"Grandson," I murmur, remembering stories from my father. "He was the boss's grandson."

"And he has a taste for the mob," Cox says. "I don't know who Pavlov pissed off, but it filtered to Carlito, and that is what spurred the search for Ivie. They thought they could hurt the old man if they got their hands on his daughter."

"Little do they know that Pavlov doesn't give two

fucks about Ivie," Nadia says, fury shooting from her gorgeous blue eyes.

"Are Carlito and Sergi working together?" I wonder aloud. "I want to know *exactly* what Billy knows. That piece of shit."

I want to punch something. Hard.

"Okay, we're going to go about this methodically." Rocco turns from the window where he's been taking it all in. "I'm headed to Dallas in the morning."

"Nadia and I will go to New York," Carmine says. "I already have a rapport with Billy. And I can just tell him that Nadia wants to shop for the wedding. I had good dealings with him just a couple of months ago."

"Good." I tap my fingers on the desk. "I'm not going to just sit on the ranch anymore. It's not safe. I should have left last night, but I didn't have this information yet."

"Leaving is a good idea," Cameron says with a nod. "Get her to Seattle."

"He's right." Carmine stands. "Take her to Gram's house. The security is brand new, the house is secluded, and it's not under your name. Not to mention, it has the safe room in the basement."

I nod, thinking it over. "It's the best solution. We'll be ready to go by this evening."

"I'll fly you over before I go to Dallas," Rocco says. "It's not exactly on my way, but I'd like to be the pilot for that trip."

"Appreciate it."

"I'm done," Cameron says, regret in his eyes. "I can't do any more for you. I'm sorry. I'm breaking free of this life because I want a family of my own. I want Mary Margaret. And I want to make sure she's safe."

"You've done more than enough." I shake my friend's hand. "Thank you. I want an invitation to the wedding."

"I have to talk her into marrying me first." He grins. "You'll get one. You all will. Good luck, and be careful."

He waves and shuts the door behind him, leaving me alone with my family.

"I'm fucking pissed," I growl.

"Are you angry because they're threatening *someone* or because they're trying to kill the woman you love?" Carmine wonders.

"I won't deny it. I love her. I won't let them hurt her. And I'm going to kill them all."

Carmine nods. Rocco cracks his knuckles.

"We'll help," Nadia says as she stands. "It's time we teach the Sergis a lesson."

I TEXTED Curt when I left Denver to let him know I'd be back home shortly. I hit some fucking traffic just outside of the city, which lost me about thirty minutes, but I'm now getting close to the ranch.

Cell service is spotty on this section of road, but suddenly a text comes through from Curt.

Curt: *12 to 20 operatives. Breached from the west.*

"Fuck. Fuck, fuck, fuck." I hit the steering wheel. I should have listened to Curt and my gut last night and gotten the hell out of there.

Instead, Ivie and Curt are both in harm's way.

I slow the vehicle and snarl when I see four Jeeps pulled into the bushes on the edge of my property.

I pull in behind them, arm myself with a knife and two pistols, and make a mental note of where I have weapons hidden on the property. No one, not even Curt, knows that I've got at least ten stashes of weapons placed strategically.

I ease out of my vehicle and silently creep up on a man who's standing by the Jeep in front. He's looking at his phone.

He's an idiot. These people need to hire better lookouts.

I easily sneak up on him and slit his throat, then let him fall to the ground.

One down. I have no idea when Curt sent that text since I'm often in dead zones between Denver and the ranch. I don't know if he's already taken out a good portion of the men, if they've killed him, or even if they've reached Ivie.

Fuck, I'm going in blind.

I take a deep breath and walk, low and fast, through the invisible fence and up a short hill to survey the scene.

I see two men, pacing back and forth, each armed

with automatic weapons. These two have more training, watching the area around them closely.

I pull my sidearm from its holster, screw on the silencer, and shoot them both in the forehead before they can blink.

Three down.

I hurry over to the bodies, relieve them of their weapons, and crouch, listening.

I hear voices to the east but no gunfire. No struggles.

Staying close to the ground, I hurry on. When I see the door to the bunker, I blow out a breath of relief when I see the discreet green light level with the ground.

That means someone is inside. Safe. It hasn't been breached. Praying that it's Ivie in there, I continue, moving toward the house, and see movement on my right.

It's Curt, cutting a man's throat very much the same way I just did back at the Jeeps.

I start to wave him down, but he sees movement and throws the knife, hitting another man square in the forehead, killing him instantly.

I don't ever want to be on Curt's bad side.

I issue the low whistle we used to use back in the day and nod when Curt's gaze finds mine. I see his shoulders relax, and then he starts giving me hand signals.

Eight more men on the property. Four at the house, four at the barn.

I nod and silently give him directions to go to the barn, indicating I'll take the house.

He nods in affirmation, and we set off to find our targets. I crouch in the long grass and quickly type out a message to Rocco.

Me: *Infiltrated. Need the chopper to get out ASAP.*

I don't wait for a reply as I hurry to the house. I don't see any movement outside, so I press my back against the wall and ease over to look in a window.

Two men in the kitchen.

I keep going around the house, looking in the windows. The basement door is still secure. That's a good sign.

I move to the side door, near a sunroom that I've never furnished, and see two more men about to come outside.

So, I wait for them. Let them come to me. If I can eliminate them without using a firearm, all the better. I don't want to alert the two inside.

With my back to the side of the house, I wait while the two come through the squeaky screen door, and when they come around the corner, I spring into action. The first one gets his neck broken, and then I spin and wrap my legs around the other's neck, taking him to the ground. I fling my arm back and stab him in the neck.

Seven down. There are two more here, and four with Curt.

I slink into the house, silently moving through the rooms, my weapon drawn.

Both of the remaining men are bent over the basement door lock, trying to disarm it and get inside.

Morons.

I'm able to sidle up behind them and look down at the doorknob.

"How's it going?" I ask, surprising them.

Before they can draw their weapons, I have them both on the ground, dead.

No blood.

That would be messy to clean up.

I check for pulses before opening the basement door and slinking down the stairs to look at the monitors. I check the bunker first.

Ivie's there, watching the other wall of monitors. Good, she's safe.

Then I check the barn. I count three dead bodies. None of them are Curt, but I can't locate him. After scanning the rest of the screens, I don't see any other men on the property.

Just Curt and one remaining asshole.

I shut it all down, hurry up the stairs, lock the door behind me, and am out of the house and running to the barn within seconds.

When I reach the building, I stop to listen.

I hear a scuffle coming from the side of the structure.

I run toward it, my weapon drawn once again, and find Curt punching the fuck out of a man. He has blood coming from his nose, but he's spouting profanities.

"Don't kill him," I instruct in a firm, cold voice. Curt immediately stops punching but holds the asshole against the building.

"Who do you work for?" I demand.

The piece of shit spits in my face.

"That's not the answer I wanted. Curt?"

Curt takes his knife and slices off the man's ear, making him squeal like a pig.

"Now, let's try that again. Who do you work for?"

"You're just going to kill me." He's not wrong. "I'm not telling you shit."

"All of your comrades are dead. All of them. Now, we can make this easy on you, and I can kill you fast—you won't feel anything. *If* you answer the question. If you don't, I can make your last few minutes as miserable and painful as anyone has ever been through. It's up to you."

His eyes fill with tears, his lip quivers.

"Billy Sergi."

"Not his father?"

"I take my orders from Billy."

I nod thoughtfully. "Is anyone else on their way?"

"He hired us to handle it. We're military-trained. How you two killed us all, I'll never know."

"Whoever trained you should be ashamed." I push my face close to his. "I'm going to be the one to end you. And Billy. And anyone else who tries to kill her."

And with that, I press the barrel of my sidearm against his temple and pull the trigger.

CHAPTER 15

~IVIE~

"What is taking them so long?" I pull at my hair and pace the dark bunker. I've never been more relieved in my life as I was when Shane came on camera. And then, when he and Curt systematically killed every single one of those men, all I could do was watch with my jaw dropped.

I have *so* many questions for the man I've completely fallen in love with.

But first, I need him to come get me. I promised that I wouldn't leave this bunker until someone came to get me.

So, where the fuck are they?

I hurry back to look at the monitors and almost squeal in delight when I see Shane walking toward the bunker door.

I run to the stairs, and when he opens the door, I launch myself into his arms and hold on tight.

"Oh, God. Oh, God. You're okay."

"I'm okay." His arms tighten around me. "You stayed put."

"I'm not stupid." I cup his face in my hands and kiss him hard. "Shit, that was scary. Is Curt okay?"

"He's fine."

I glance over Shane's shoulder at the sound of Curt's voice.

"I have so many questions," I reply.

"No time," Shane says and sets me on the floor. "We all need to pack a bag and be ready to leave in ten minutes. Rocco's on the way with the chopper."

I'm relieved. I want to get the hell out of here.

"I should stay." Curt hooks his thumbs in his jeans and shakes his head. "Someone needs to be here to make sure everything's okay."

"It's not safe," Shane says, his voice leaving no room for argument. "You're coming with us."

"Shane—"

"I mean it. I need you with us, not here like a sitting duck. We're headed to Seattle. When everything is over, we'll come back."

"Let's just hope there's something to come back to," Curt mutters but hurries away without more argument.

"Come on. Let's grab what you need and get out of here."

"You'll get no complaint from me," I reply and have to hurry to keep up with Shane's long strides. I'm short, and I don't run—unless something's chasing me.

And right now, something is definitely chasing me.

"Shane, I want to talk."

"We'll have plenty of time in Seattle," he assures me and seems to move faster as we approach the house. "There are bodies inside, baby. I'm sorry. I don't have time to clean them up."

"I'll be okay." I take a deep breath. "Are you just going to leave them here?"

"A cleanup crew will come in later today and get rid of them."

I stop and stare at him. "A *cleanup* crew?"

"That's right. Now, hurry up and grab what you need. I'm headed down to close up the basement."

"Want me to grab some stuff for you, too?"

"That would be great."

He pats my ass, and then he's stomping down the stairs, and I'm running to the bedroom.

I find my mama's suitcase, and it only takes a few seconds to throw my clothes inside. Then I make a quick run through the bathroom to gather my things and Shane's, too.

By the time he rushes into the bedroom, I have our bags packed.

"You're fast," he says.

"This isn't the first time I've had to do this."

I can hear the helicopter as Shane tips up my chin. "I know. I'm sorry, honey."

"Let's get out of here."

I refuse to look at the men dead on the floor as we run out of the house and join Curt at the helicopter.

Rafe doesn't bother jumping out. We all climb in, put headsets on, and buckle up.

"Ready?" Rafe's voice says in my ear. Shane and Curt give him a thumbs up, and I follow suit, and then we're rising above the Earth, and my stomach does a flip.

I hate rides. I usually get sick. But all I can think about is getting out of here.

I see bodies scattered on the earth. And then I just see trees as Rocco picks up speed, and we're suddenly flying over the mountains.

"The plane is ready in Denver," Rafe says. "We'll leave as soon as we get there and set out for Seattle."

"Can I see Annika?" I ask, speaking for the first time. "She'll worry, and I'm not allowed to call her."

"Don't worry," Shane says, taking my hand. "We'll figure out a way for you to speak with her."

I nod, bite my lip, and look out the window, doing my best not to cry. Now that the adrenaline is wearing off, I just want to sob.

And maybe sleep for a week.

Shane puts his hand on my thigh and gives it a squeeze, but I can't look over at him.

He's safe.

Curt's fine.

We got out.

But, damn, I'm still so scared. And what if we get to Seattle, and it doesn't stop? We can't run forever. I can't ask these people to keep putting their lives on hold and continue putting themselves at risk.

Something has to give.

I have to talk to Shane about all of this. I need to know more about him. I need more, period. He must have more information after speaking with Cameron earlier today.

Was that just today? It feels like a million years ago.

Denver comes into view, and soon, we're descending to a helipad.

"I thought we were going to the airport?" I ask, confused.

"This is a smaller airfield. For private aircraft," Rafe says and makes the landing look *so* easy. The hatch opens, and we hustle out of the chopper and hurry over to the waiting plane.

When I climb the stairs and duck inside, I'm shocked to find Carmine, Nadia, and *Annika* already seated.

"Oh, my God. What are you doing here?"

"Rafe seems to think I'm in danger," she says as I cross the space and sit next to her. Rafe, who's just come in behind me, scowls at my best friend.

"You *are* in danger," he says. "She was taken from *your* clinic. She's *your* best friend. I don't need one of these assholes coming in to try and get information from you. You're coming with us, where we can keep you safe."

Annika blows out a breath, rolls her eyes, and turns to me.

"See what I've been dealing with? And that was all over the phone. Now that he's here in person, he'll just glare at me all day."

I feel my eyes fill with tears. I didn't know until this moment how badly I needed my best friends.

Nadia sits on my other side and takes my hand, and I lay my head on Annika's shoulder.

The tears come now. Big, hot tears that I've been holding inside. They just burst out of me, and all I can do is hang onto my friends for dear life.

They know me, inside and out. They know *everything.*

And they love me.

When the tears have dried up, and all I can do is sit and rest, someone offers me a glass of water.

"Remember Charles?" Shane says from across the aisle, watching me with sober brown eyes.

"You need some water, miss," Charles says. "And I'm happy to bring you anything else you might need."

"I could go for some pizza," I mutter. "And choco-late ice cream."

"We'll make sure you get that when we get settled." Nadia pats my arm.

"Can I offer you some cheese and crackers? Some fruit?" Charles asks.

"That would be nice." I nod and sit up straight, pushing my hair back over my shoulders. "Sorry, everyone. The day just caught up to me."

"No apologies necessary," Carmine says. "You've had a hell of a day."

"All I did was sit in a bunker and watch Shane and Curt—" I shake my head. "I didn't do much."

"You kept yourself safe," Nadia says and kisses my cheek. "That's a lot."

"Your grandmother had a beautiful house," I say three hours later after we've landed in Seattle and made our way to the mansion we'd be staying in for the foreseeable future. It's a fortress of a house, which I would expect from the Martinellis.

A massive manor in the middle of manicured lawns with fountains and shrubberies. It was a bit intimidating when we drove up.

Then slipped over into ridiculously intimidating when we walked through the door. I've only seen tapestries in movies. The antiques are incredible. And yet, despite the grandeur of the home, it's incredibly modern and comfortable.

"Gram liked nice things," Shane says as he leads me on a tour through the home. "But she also liked to be comfortable, so she managed to keep it updated. The kitchen is less than five years old."

I nod and then follow Shane up a flight of stairs.

"All of the bedrooms are on this floor. Eight of them altogether."

"Geez."

He grins at me. "I know. It's a lot. Our room is at the end, with the pond out back. You can see where our treehouse is, and the view is especially pretty in the morning."

I don't say much when he opens the door, and I follow him in. The bed looks comfortable. And expensive.

The attached bathroom boasts a tub big enough to swim in.

I'll be more than comfortable here.

"This is great. Thank you."

"Okay, I've had it." He closes the door and pulls me into his arms, holding me tightly. "You're quiet, your eyes are haunted, and you're scaring me. What are you thinking?"

I want to cry again. "I don't know. It's just a lot, you know?"

"I know." He kisses my head. "I'm so sorry, babe. This is a safe place."

"We thought the ranch was safe." I swallow hard and back out of his arms. "I think I should look at going out on my own."

His eyes flash, and he starts to shake his head, but I hold up a hand.

"Hear me out. They're finding me because they

know I'm with *you*. With the Martinellis and the Tarenkovs. They'll keep tracking down you and your family, Annika, to find me. That's not fair to anyone, Shane. It's not right."

"Ivie."

"I've disappeared before," I remind him. "And I was a lot younger with little education. Now, I can hack into anything, change my name again, and start over. I can go anywhere. I'm smarter, and I have a little money saved up to get started."

"No."

I pace away from him, my mind forming around the idea.

"I mean, I'll miss you all. Never seeing Annika and Nadia again might kill me, but if it keeps you all safe, it's the right thing to do."

"No."

"Shane, be reasonable."

"You going out on your own with some idiotic idea of keeping *us* safe is not being reasonable, Ivie. It's fucking stupid."

"I am *not* stupid."

"I didn't think so either until about thirty seconds ago. I don't need you to keep me safe."

"Yeah, I saw that on the monitors."

That makes his jaw clench, and his eyes narrow.

"Who *are* you? I keep asking and asking, and you always blow me off. If you don't want anything to do with me, fine. You don't need to tell me. But we're *sleeping* together, Shane, and you can't convince me that it's just sex. It's not. So, don't even try to say it is."

"It's not just sex," he mutters and rubs his hand over the back of his neck.

"Then I need you to *talk* to me. Because I feel that you care about me, and I sure as hell care about you. Jesus, I *need* you all to stay safe. I don't know everything that's happening, and that means that I'm scared and frustrated, and you're asking me to just blindly trust that you have everything under control."

"I *do* have everything under control. Why can't you just trust me on this and let me do my damn job?"

"Because I don't know what your job is!" I round on him, aggravation coming out of every pore on my body. "I don't know what Cameron said. I don't know *anything* except that I watched you and Curt systematically assassinate at least a dozen men today, men who were after *me*. And now you're trying to just tuck me away in this beautiful ivory tower while the menfolk take on the bad guys."

He sighs. "What do you want to know?"

"Everything!" I push my hair off my face. "I want to know everything. I think I have the right to that, Shane."

"Okay." He blows out a breath. "Curt and I *are* trained assassins. We kill people for a living for the US government. Well, he used to. He's retired."

"But you're not."

His eyes are cold and level with mine. "No. I'm not. And I can't tell you more because it's classified."

"Who do you kill?"

"Whomever they tell me to."

I swallow hard. "What did Cameron say?"

"The Sergis are behind this. The last guy we killed at the ranch confirmed he was working for them. Carmine and Nadia are planning to go to New York, where the Sergi family is based, to do some digging."

"That's it?"

He nods. "Yes."

"And now I'm just supposed to sit here and wait again?"

"I don't know what else you'd like to do. You're definitely not going to New York."

"I don't want to go to that godforsaken city ever again." I sink onto the side of the bed, suddenly bone-tired. "At least if I left, went out on my own, I'd have something to *do* and it would keep you safe."

"I'm not the one in danger," he reminds me, and the scene from just a few hours ago clearly comes to mind.

"I beg to differ."

"If you left, I would find you. And not in a creepy serial killer way."

That makes me smile, but I bite my lip, trying to stay serious.

"I didn't intend for you to come to mean so much to me, Ivie, but you do. You matter. You matter more than anything else in my life, and you going anywhere that I can't find you isn't an option for me. I know it's fast and that we have a lot to talk through when we get this all figured out. But I'm not letting you leave me."

He gently drags a fingertip down my cheek.

"I need this to be over." My voice is a hoarse whisper. "It's too much. I don't deserve this, Shane."

"I know." He pulls me into his strong arms and holds on tight. "I know. We're going to figure it out. Together."

I nod and take a deep breath. "Do you think the pizza is here yet?"

"Let's go find out."

CHAPTER 16

"*Y*ou look really good for a girl who survived a war zone this afternoon," Annika says to Ivie, who's sitting beside me in the family room, balancing a plate of pizza on her lap. "How are you holding up, honey?"

"I'm fine." Ivie sighs and takes another bite of Hawaiian pizza. "I feel like it was all a movie and that it didn't really happen. But it did."

"And now it's over," I assure her, but want to wince when she looks up at me with wide, blue eyes.

"No, it's not over."

"It will be," Nadia assures her. "Sooner than later, even if I have to kill every one of them myself."

"Let's talk about something less violent," Annika suggests, making the rest of us laugh. "I've been thinking about getting a puppy."

"What kind?" Ivie asks, sitting forward. "I want one,

too. Let's get siblings from the same litter, and they can be besties."

"Oh my gosh, *yes*," Annika agrees with excitement. "I was thinking a Shih Tzu. Or a Bichon. You know, something small and cute."

"A chick dog," Rocco says with a smirk.

"It's a *small* dog," Annika says and sends my brother a glare. "Because I don't have time to exercise a big dog, and a small dog can go to the office with me. Why do you care, anyway?"

"I literally said three words," Rocco says.

"Well, maybe you shouldn't say any words at all, Rafe Martinelli."

"Rocco," he corrects her, and Carmine and I share a look. He'll never win this battle with these women. Never.

"I will not call you *Rocco*," Annika reminds him. "Your mother named you Rafe. Your name is *Rafe*."

"Seriously, dude, Rafe is so much better," Nadia says. "I've never understood the Rocco thing."

"It's *my* name, and I can decide what I want people to call me," my brother says. "If you call me Rafe, I won't reply."

"Fine," Annika says. "I don't want to talk to you anyway so that works just fine."

"Why are you so difficult?" Rocco demands.

"You two are so cute," Ivie says with a dreamy look on her face. "The way you tease and flirt is adorable.

Why don't you just go ahead and start making out, right here."

Both Rocco and Annika glare at Ivie, which only makes us all laugh harder. These two have been fighting whatever is between them for years. And they hid it. I was shocked to discover earlier this year that they'd had a secret relationship years before. I've asked Rocco to tell me about it, but he just clams up.

He won't speak of it.

It's baffling.

"Yes, my annoyance is cute," Annika says, sarcasm dripping from every word.

"It is," Ivie insists. "If you didn't give a shit, you'd ignore him. But you do give a shit. And I don't know why you're fighting it so damn hard. But that's none of my business. I guess I was just reminded today how short life can be. And what's the point of denying what you love? What you enjoy?"

"This is getting *really* philosophical," Nadia says as she rises to her feet and wanders into the kitchen, then opens the freezer to find the ice cream. "I'm scooping up ice cream for this talk. And pouring wine. Wine and ice cream."

"I'll pour the whiskey," I offer and pour myself, Curt, and each of my brothers three fingers. Curt's sitting at the edge of the room, looking uncomfortable. Which isn't unusual when he's in a room full of people.

But he knows my family.

"Drink this." I pass him the glass and pat his shoulder. "You more than earned it today."

"I won't turn it down," he says and takes a sip. "I think I'll turn in, man. Helluva day. And I need to look over the cameras at the ranch, make sure everything is as it should be."

"Appreciate it. Let me know if you need anything. Otherwise, I'll plan to meet with you at oh-eight-hundred."

"I'll be there." He stands with his glass, nods at everyone in the room, and starts to leave, but Ivie calls out to him.

"Curt!" She jumps off the couch and hurries across the room, throwing her arms around him. "Thank you. Thank you *so much*."

"Hey." He pats her back uncomfortably and looks at me with panic in his eyes. "Don't cry."

"You saved me," she says and sniffs loudly. "And I just think you're wonderful."

"Uh, you're pretty great yourself."

I move in to rescue him, and he passes a weepy Ivie over to me. She buries her face against my chest, and I wrap my arms around her.

"Goodnight, everyone," Curt says and leaves the room.

"I know I sound stupid," Ivie says as she pulls back and wipes her eyes. "But when it all started to go down, we didn't know where Shane was, and Curt was with me. We'd just finished target practice in the firing range and were putting things away, cleaning up, when the alarms went off. Thank *God* that's where we were so he could grab weapons. I took some, too, and he made me go through the tunnel to the bunker and wait. Made me promise not to come out, under any circumstances."

She sits on the couch again and wipes her eyes. Annika passes her some tissues.

"I know you wanted to talk about less violent things—"

"It's okay," Annika assures her before I can. "Talk it out, honey."

Ivie nods. "I found the monitors in the bunker, and I could watch what was happening on the property. It was *so* crazy. Scary as hell. And then I saw Shane, and for a second, I was relieved that he was there to help, but also so fucking terrified that one of those bastards would h-h-hurt him."

I take her hand, link my fingers with hers, and raise her hand to my mouth.

"But they didn't get hurt. They saved me. And now I'm here, in Seattle, eating ice cream and pizza with my favorite people."

"I'm touched," Rocco says, making her grin.

"You're one of my favorite people, too, *Rafe.*"

My brother scowls. "I can't win with these women."

"Get used to it," Carmine suggests, earning a glare from his fiancée. "I mean that in the nicest way possible, of course."

"Sure, you do." Nadia stands and stretches. "We should go home where I can punish you for that. Let these guys get some rest."

"You're not staying here?" Ivie asks.

"Our house isn't far away," Nadia assures her. "I'll be back in the morning. I'm bringing breakfast. Then Carmine and I are headed to New York for a few days."

"I don't like it," Ivie says, blowing out a breath.

"Don't worry. We'll be fine." Nadia hugs Ivie close. "I'll see you in the morning.

Carmine and Nadia say their goodbyes, but Rocco hangs back.

"I'm staying," he says simply and looks at Annika. "My room is next to yours. If you need *anything*, just let me know."

"I—" Annika begins, but Rocco cuts her off.

"Don't argue, just say 'okay.'"

"Okay," she replies. "Thanks."

He nods and walks out of the room.

"He really does worry about you," I say to Annika.

"I know." She sighs and offers me a small smile. "I've worked really hard for a while now to distance myself from him and my feelings for him. Old habits die hard. I'm going up, too. But I suspect I'll be back for another glass of wine."

"Take the bottle," Ivie suggests. "I'll sneak over and drink it with you."

"You don't have to sneak." I grin at her.

"Even better."

"WE HAVEN'T HEARD ANYTHING."

Ivie and I are walking across the grass of my grand-mother's property. It's been three days since we arrived. Carmine and Nadia are wrapping things up in New York, and Rocco is on his way back from Texas. He left yesterday morning.

He didn't want to be away from Annika for too long.

Even though the woman pretends that she can't stand the sight of him.

"Everyone will be back by morning," I assure Ivie.

"But I don't know what they found. Where did Rafe go, anyway?"

"He just had some work to do, some things to see to. I suspect we'll have information from all of them tomorrow."

"I hope so. We've been here for three days, and nothing is happening. It's quiet. Which I'm not complaining about because I've been up close and personal with the alternative and I'll take quiet over that every time. But I don't trust it."

I don't either. There hasn't been any chatter, nothing to report. It's too quiet again.

I don't like it.

"Let's enjoy the sunshine today and worry about the rest when the others get here tomorrow," I suggest.

"You're right. It's a nice day. Tomorrow is Annika's birthday, and I haven't had time to get her anything."

"I'm quite sure she understands."

Ivie smiles. "You're right. I'll figure something out for her. It's pretty out here. You said you spent a good portion of your childhood here?"

"Yes. This was my father's parents' home. We came here every summer, along with our cousin, Elena. Ran wild all over this property. Swam in the pond, played in the gazebo. Gram had that treehouse built when Carmine was about eight."

I point to the treehouse ahead. I'm taking her there. It's private, and I plan to talk to her. Tell her how I feel —how much I love her, and that I want to make this work between us. She's right, life is short, too damn short, and I'm going to hold onto her for as long as I possibly can.

"I can picture it," she says with a smile. "It's a great property for kids."

"And Gram spoiled us rotten. She had a firm hand, and we didn't get anything by her, but she gave us just about anything we wanted. The entire top floor of the house is an attic, and we loved to play up there. She never threw anything away."

"I bet it's a treasure trove."

"It is. She's been gone more than a year now, and we haven't had time to go through everything yet. But she'd be happy that we're using the house."

"And your parents? Are they close by?"

"Yes. Actually, my father will be here tomorrow to meet with my brothers and me. My mom might come with him. You'll get to meet them."

"I've met them," she says with a soft smile. "At Annika's wedding. I've seen them from afar here and there over the years."

I look down at her in surprise. "I don't remember meeting you before that wedding."

"I don't think we met. Not formally, anyway. I was just around now and then at parties the families were invited to."

"No way. I would have noticed you."

"No, you wouldn't." Ivie shakes her head and then laughs. "I'm not the type of girl that men notice, Shane."

"We've been over this. I think you're hot. So, if you were around, I would have noticed."

She smiles up at me as we approach the treehouse. "Well, we're here now, and that's all that really matters."

"I'm excited to show this to you. I'll go first and make sure it's still sound."

"Please don't fall through rotted wood," she says and watches as I climb the ladder. When I arrive at the top, I'm pleased to see that everything is as sound as it was the day it was built, almost thirty years ago.

"It's good." I look down at her. "Come on up."

"Are you sure?"

"Totally sure. Solid as a rock."

She climbs up the rungs and takes my proffered hand to pull herself up to the platform.

"It's bigger than it looks," she says.

"That's what she said."

She frowns at me, slaps my arm, and then giggles. "Okay, that was funny. But seriously, it's really spacious up here."

"We used to have furniture and all kinds of crap, but it got thrown away a long time ago. It was just a squirrel magnet and would have rotted this place quick. So, it's just sitting here empty."

"I like it." She paces around the space, walks to a window and looks out over the green grass, the pond, and the house. "You got to grow up here."

"Yeah. Pretty great, huh?"

"Pretty great." She nods and turns to me. "How many girls have you brought up here over the years?"

I grin and rub my chin as if giving it a lot of thought. "Man, at least…one. Just you."

She cocks a brow, and her eyes shine in approval. "I think we should have sex. Right here."

And just like that, all of my thoughts of romantic words and confessions flee my brain, and my cock is fully alert.

"Is that right?"

She nods and backs away from the window, pulling her skirt up around her hips, then letting her panties fall to the floor. "Yeah. I'm not gonna get naked because I don't want splinters in my back."

"Good plan, babe." I unzip my pants and cross to her, pinning her against the wall as I take my time kissing the ball of her shoulder, then up her neck to nibble on her earlobe.

"I don't want it to be slow." Her breath is airy now and catches when my fingers slide up the inside of her thigh to her wet center. "I want you to fuck me, right here, against the wall of your treehouse."

"It would be rude of me to tell you no."

She laughs, and then I boost her up, her legs encircling my hips as I drive into her, making us both gasp. Her mouth gapes as I sit there, buried deep, staring into her eyes.

"Mine," I whisper.

"Yours." She clenches. "Move, Shane. Fuck me."

I tip my brow to hers and can't resist her. My hips move faster and faster. With the way I'm pounding into her, it's a damn good thing this thing is sturdy, or we'd be on the ground, twenty feet below.

Her fists clench in my hair, and she moans, long and low, as she comes around me. The ripples are fierce and nearly coax an orgasm from me.

My God, I'm lost in her. In every way.

And I'm never letting her go.

"Again." I pull out, set her feet on the floor, and turn her away from me. "Grab the wall and hold on."

I easily slide back inside and take us both on another ride. Her round ass is perfect in my hands as I take her from behind. I grip the hair on the back of her head and push us both harder, faster than before.

The second orgasm is more powerful than the first,

and when we've finally caught our breath, all I can do is pull her to me and hold on.

"I should have had a bed brought up here."

She chuckles against my chest. "That wouldn't have been obvious at all."

"Who cares what anyone thinks?" I tip her chin up and kiss her long and slow.

"I couldn't agree more."

CHAPTER 17

~IVIE~

"This is the *best* way to spend a birthday," Annika says with a long, luxurious sigh. We're lounging in a massive sunroom, with a water fountain trickling not far away. The lounge chairs are plush and comfortable enough to fall asleep in. And all three of us, Nadia, Annika, and me, are being pampered. "I can't believe you brought the spa here."

"We can't go to the spa," Nadia says and sips her mimosa, "so why not bring them to us? Oh, here, I chose the red polish for my toes."

Nadia passes her nail tech the polish and then grins over at me.

I don't remember the last time I felt this *relaxed.* My toes are freshly painted pink, I've had a massage and a facial, and just finished eating the *best* salad I've ever had in my life. And now I'm sitting with my best friends, drinking mimosas. It feels like the old times.

"I want to marry that masseuse," Annika says with a wink. "He had *very* good hands."

"Raul is amazing," the nail tech says with a grin. "And is my husband."

"You're a lucky woman." Annika laughs.

"I think Rafe would be unhappy if you married the masseuse," I say and slide a sly look over at my best friend. "I noticed he went directly to your room when he got back last night."

Annika shifts in her seat and reaches to refill her glass. "He was just checking in."

"Are you ever going to give him a chance?" Nadia demands. "You're not married anymore. I know Rich has only been dead for, like, three months, but there's no love lost there."

The nail tech clears her throat and tightens the lid on her portable caddy. "Ladies, I think we're done here. It was a pleasure to meet you all."

"Thank you," we all say in unison. Nadia and the woman exchange a couple of words about the bill, and then we're alone in the sunroom. "I think I might have scared her when I mentioned that your husband is dead."

"I thought she was going to choke." I shake my head and then giggle. "Anyway, the point is still valid. Rich was a grade-A dick, and he's gone. There's no reason you can't start something with Rafe."

"Rafe isn't meant for me," Annika insists.

"You're so fucking stubborn." I sit up and turn to

face my friend. "It's not every day that a girl meets a guy who looks at her the way Rafe looks at you."

"Oh, you mean the way Shane looks at *you*?" Annika counters. "Tell us what's going on there."

"You're changing the subject."

Nadia and Annika just lean in closer, waiting for me to answer.

"Fine. Shane is awesome. The sex is off the charts. He's attentive and sweet, and sometimes maddening. But, hey, who isn't, right?"

"Carmine drives me up the fucking wall," Nadia agrees. "Have you said the L-word yet?"

"No." I sigh and stand to pace the room, but when I almost trip and fall into the fountain, I return to my chair where it's safe. "There are…issues."

"Honey, you don't get past the age of sixteen and not have issues," Annika reminds me. "I mean, I know that yours are heavier than most, but you've come a long way since that girl in New York."

"Not just my stuff—of which there is legion—but he has stuff, too. And I don't think Shane is convinced that he *deserves* to have someone in his life long-term, you know? He's told me a bit of what his job is, and that coupled with his family and all of those responsibilities…I think he's resigned to being alone. And that's sad."

"You're in love with him." Annika's statement leaves no room for argument. And I don't want to deny it.

"I am." I prop my chin in my hand and sigh. "I mean,

have you seen his muscles? And that smile? And when he gets really intense, his brown eyes get this edge to them that makes me want to just *bite* him."

"Carmine has the same eyes," Nadia says with a nod.

"So does Rafe, except his are blue." Annika blinks when we just stare at her. "What? They're brothers."

"Anyway, we'll figure it out, one way or the other. I just hope I don't end up with a broken heart because that will suck."

"If he breaks your heart, I'll break his kneecaps," Nadia says.

"You're scary sometimes." I pour more mimosas for all of us. "Sometimes, like now, it's easy to forget that you're a badass bratva princess."

"Honey, I'm a queen." Nadia's grin is sassy and confident.

"I want to be Nadia when I grow up," I declare as I raise my glass to my lips. "Now, tell us about the wedding plans."

"We're going to have it here. At this house."

"Oh, that's a great idea," Annika says. "The grounds are just gorgeous."

"Yeah, and Carmine was really close with his grandmother, so I think it's a nice tribute to her." Nadia shrugs a shoulder. "My father is fine with it, which kind of surprised me given that our families haven't always been besties, but things are better now."

"Do you have a dress?" I ask. "I hate that this whole

mess has happened while you're planning, and that I haven't been able to go with you."

"Neither of us has," Annika says. "I'm sorry."

"Actually, I have twenty dresses arriving here from New York in about an hour. I need help. So, they're coming to us."

"God, it's good to be rich." I sit back and grin at my friend. "You lucky bitch."

"It has its perks." Nadia raises her glass. "Oh, and Carmine's mom is coming to help. My mom will join us via FaceTime."

"Well, let's go get ready, then."

"DARLING!" Flavia Martinelli bursts into the massive room that's been converted into a dressing room, her arms outstretched. She engulfs Nadia in a big hug. "You're as gorgeous as ever. I'm so grateful that you invited me here today to see the dresses."

The Martinelli matriarch is tall, slender, and shrewd. Carlo married an attractive and clever woman, who raised three boys, is submerged in her community, and keeps an eye on the who's who of Seattle's elite.

She's known for being a force to be reckoned with. She's always been kind to me, and I have to admit, I admire her for her style, and her sense of humor.

Then again, I suspect one would need to have one to be a boss's wife.

"Hello, girls," she says, turning to Annika and me. "I haven't had a girls' day in...I can't even remember. I'm always surrounded by men."

"Good-looking men at that," Annika reminds her.

"Well, that doesn't hurt, now does it?" Flavia winks and accepts a glass of champagne. "Oh, how lovely. I'm so excited. Get your gorgeous body into a dress, Nadia."

"Okay. First, let me get my mom on the computer."

"Oh, how wonderful," Flavia says and claps her hands. "Katya and I spoke just last night about wedding plans. We're just beside ourselves with excitement."

I sit back and watch as Nadia gets her mother on screen, and Flavia and Annika share a smile.

And I can't help but grieve, for just a moment.

I won't ever have this moment with my mother. Someone stole that from me. And I can't make the person who took her from me pay for that sin. I can't help but feel a little envious that Nadia has this with her mom.

Of course, I'm also excited for her. And when Katya sees me, she grins and waves.

"Hello, Ivie, my darling girl. You look just as beautiful as can be."

"Thank you, Mrs. Tarenkov."

"I'm here, too," Annika says, waving to her. "Hello, Aunt Katya."

"Oh, Annika, you're as lovely as always. Who else is there?"

"It's me, Katie dear." Flavia smiles at the computer. "I wish you were here with us."

"Well, give me just a minute."

Suddenly, the door opens, and Katya walks into the room, opens her arms wide, and starts to laugh.

"Did you think I'd watch this on a small, pitiful screen?"

"Mama!" Nadia rushes over and hugs her mother. The room erupts into chaos as we all shriek and laugh and hug each other in delight.

Carmine pokes his head in the doorway, grinning. "Surprise."

"I love you." Nadia crushes her mouth to his. "Now, get out of here. You can't see any of this. It's for girls only."

"I'll have food sent up in about thirty minutes. Have fun, ladies."

He shuts the door behind him, and we all settle in for the fashion show.

"Oh, this is just the best day," Flavia says as she clasps Katya's hands. "How lovely."

Before long, Nadia walks into the room wearing a long column of white. It hugs her curves, has just a hint of lace, and is absolutely gorgeous.

She steps up onto the pedestal that the fashion house brought with them as a woman named Lydia fluffs the trumpet skirt.

"Now, that is gorgeous," Annika breathes. "The back is *stunning.*"

I tilt my head, not convinced that it's the right one.

"Oh, Flavia," Katya says. "Can you imagine the pretty grandchildren we'll get?"

"Mom." Nadia rolls her eyes. "I'm not having babies."

"Nonsense." Katya brushes the comment away with the flip of her hand. "Turn this way, please. What do you think?"

"It's not me," Nadia replies. It's pretty, but I don't like the lace. No lace."

"Okay, let's try again." Lydia smiles and gestures for Nadia to follow her to the changing room.

Two hours, ten dresses, three glasses of champagne, and six finger sandwiches later, Nadia has tears in her eyes as she stares at herself in the mirror.

"Oh, darling," Flavia breathes. "Carmine will lose his ever-loving mind."

"He'll pass right out," I agree.

"I met him at a wedding," Nadia whispers. "When I was twelve. And I thought he was the most handsome man I'd ever seen in my life. And now I'm *marrying* him."

Katya rests her hands on her daughter's shoulders and looks at her in the mirror. The two look so much alike with their fair hair and skin and big, blue eyes.

"You're a vision," Katya says. "Your father will blubber like a baby."

"I've never seen Papa cry."

"Well, you will on your wedding day. Is this the one?"

"Yeah, it's no contest. Now, I'd better get it off before I rip it or spill something on it."

"Such a wonderful choice," Lydia says, nodding in approval. "And this one is on the less-expensive side at only twenty-two thousand dollars."

I blink, sure I've heard her wrong. She added a zero in there somewhere. Right?

But Nadia just nods once, and says, "I'll take it."

I LOVE them all so much, but I need a few minutes of quiet. And I want to see Shane. I haven't seen him hardly at all today, and the fact that I'm having withdrawal is just another clue that I'm totally head-over-heels for the man.

I feel fantastic. My body is loose and relaxed, and I haven't laughed with my friends so much in years. Things are finally starting to look up.

I am just about to turn the corner into the kitchen when I hear Shane's voice and stay out of sight, frowning.

"I still can't believe the son of a bitch is alive."

"I remember when he was supposedly killed." That voice is Igor Tarenkov. "Many people wanted him dead."

"Yeah, Pavlov was a real piece of work," Carlo

Martinelli says. "He was on all of the families' radars. He was mostly harmless but completely untrustworthy. He was a thief and didn't even have enough honor to protect his wife and child."

"I've known that Ivie was his daughter since the day Annika brought her home from college," Igor says, surprising me. I didn't know that he knew. "I likely knew before Annika did. Ivie is a good girl. She couldn't be more different than the man who sired her. She certainly doesn't know that the man lives."

I cover my mouth, suppressing the sound of my surprised gasp. My father *is* alive? How? I saw him hanging for myself. We were so sure that the phone number we found was a cover.

Without giving it another thought, I storm into the kitchen, every nerve ending in my body radiating anger and frustration.

"What did you say?" I stare at Shane, my hands on my hips.

"Ivie, we're in a meeting—"

I step forward until I'm toe-to-toe with him. "*What* did you just say?"

"I like her," Carlo says, but I don't look his way.

"Your father is alive," Shane says.

"And how long have you known that little piece of information, Shane?"

He doesn't even have the decency to look ashamed.

"A few days."

"A *few* days? Did you know the day we arrived here

and we talked? When you fucking *swore* to me that you didn't know more?"

His nostrils flare, and I already know the answer.

"Yes. I knew then."

"I can't *believe* this. I trusted you. All of you. And you withheld this from me? What possible reason could there be for that, knowing what that monster did to me?"

"We were gathering information, little one," Igor says, and I turn to him. His eyes are full of compassion, and it's almost my undoing.

But I firm my lower lip and look around the room at a group of men I thought were being honest with me —and just feel complete betrayal.

Especially from Shane.

"Tell me more."

"I saw him with my own eyes. He goes by the name of James Peterson now," Rocco adds. "I sat in front of his house in a suburb outside of Dallas for an hour. No one came or went, but I added a camera to his mailbox, pointed at the house, just in case something interesting happens."

"Like what?" I ask.

"*Anything*," Carmine replies. "We don't know enough about him at this point to know who he's involved with or how he's been spending the past dozen years."

My father is *alive*.

That piece of shit is still allowed to breathe?

No.

"You should have told me." I glare at the man I love and turn to run out of the kitchen.

I'm too angry to stay. I'll end up saying something I regret. Instead, I run up to my bedroom and pace for a moment, and then make a snap decision.

I'm going to go find that asshole and kill him myself. This is what I've been training for, isn't it?

I quickly grab my laptop and purse and hurry down the stairs and out the front door, but stop short when I see the security guard named Peter blocking my way.

"Miss?"

"Oh, hi." I offer him a charming smile. "I was hoping I would run into you. Shane told me to find you and ask you to drive me to the airport."

He narrows his eyes. I'd better talk fast if I'm going to make him believe me.

"He's currently in a meeting with his father and the others and can't be interrupted. He said you'd take care of me."

"He said no such thing."

My eyes close at the hard voice behind me. *Shit.*

CHAPTER 18

"*W*hat do you think you're doing?" I demand when I get Ivie back inside. She's quivering with anger, and frankly, I'm just as pissed.

"I'm going to Dallas. To kill my father."

I blink at her and then shake my head. "Like hell, you are."

"Like hell, I'm *not*." She narrows those spectacular eyes on me. "You've been training me for weeks. Do you think I'm not capable of this?"

"I think you're perfectly capable, Ivie. What I won't allow is having you sneak out of here to go there *alone*."

"Oh, you won't *allow* me?" She drops her bag to the floor and crosses her arms over her chest. "Because I'm what, your *child*?"

"Now you're just pissing me off for the sake of pissing me off."

"No, I'm being an adult woman who doesn't need your permission for anything, Shane. You're not my father or my husband."

We'll be rectifying that little detail as soon as possible. But now isn't the time or place to propose.

She'd tell me to shove the ring up my ass.

"Now, excuse me. I need to go call a cab."

"No, damn it." I take her arm but quickly let go when she swings around and punches me in the jaw, just the way we taught her. "Hell."

"I'm not playing around, Shane."

"Obviously. Fine, but you're not going alone."

She starts to argue, but I've had about enough of this bullshit.

"Stop talking for two fucking minutes." I pace in a circle, frustration pulsing through me. "We'll go to Dallas, but you won't go by yourself. If you think I'd be okay with that, in any universe, you don't know me at all."

"You're right. I thought I knew you, but all you do is fucking *lie to me.*"

"Stop it. I didn't tell you because I didn't know if it was fucking true. You wondered, as well when we saw his name tied to those phone records. I wasn't going to tell you something that would change your entire world off hearsay, Ivie. We needed eyes on him. Confirmation. And *then* I was going to tell you. Today. I needed the intel from Rocco."

"I should have been in on the information from the

get-go. And then, if it wasn't true, I should have known that, too. I'm not some damsel in distress here, Shane. Now, get me to Dallas, or I'll go myself."

I want to shake her. I want her to just *listen* and try to see this from my perspective, but she's too angry.

It'll have to wait.

"We'll leave in an hour."

She turns on her heel and walks away, and I return to the kitchen, where everyone is still waiting.

"Looks like we're headed to Dallas," is all I say.

"I really like her, son," Pop says with a grin. "Keep that one."

NINETY MINUTES LATER, we're all on the jet, headed for Dallas. Even Pop and Igor decided to join.

They don't usually go into the field anymore—haven't for many years—but they wanted to come along. They'll visit a friend in Dallas while we find Pavlov.

"Do you realize what you're about to do?" I ask Ivie, who's sitting across from me. Her gaze flies to mine and holds steady.

Good girl.

"Yes."

"He isn't a stranger," I remind her, aware that all eyes are on us. Nadia watches with concern and reaches out to pat Ivie on the shoulder.

"No, he's a monster," Ivie says in a firm voice. "And he killed my mother. I've seen the photos of what he did to her. To save his own ass. And I remember, in vivid detail, the things he made me do on his behalf. He doesn't deserve to live."

I sigh and realize that I won't be able to talk her out of this. But she won't go alone.

"Blood isn't always family," Igor says, looking intently at Ivie. "Sometimes, what's born into a family is not the same. Does not belong."

I glance at Nadia, knowing full well that Igor is speaking of his son.

"And there are other times when family has no blood tie at all, and that's what we have with you, Ivie. You are one of us, and we will do everything in our power, which is considerable, to keep you safe and make sure you have your revenge."

Ivie blinks quickly, soaking in his words.

"Now, you said earlier that you thought you could trust these men, and I'm here to assure you that you *can*. But you already know that. Your anger is warranted, but make sure you focus it on the appropriate target. Shane was doing what he thought was right. Because he cares for you and doesn't want you hurt."

"I know," she whispers and blows out a breath then looks up at me. Everything we've been through together flows between us. We're going to be okay. "I know that."

"Good."

"One more thing," Nadia adds. "Don't hesitate. If you do, you won't go through with it, and you could be hurt. If your intention is to kill, don't pause. He may be an old man, but he could be dangerous. Keep your mind clear. Don't let him surprise you. I made that mistake, and it almost cost Carmine and me our lives."

Ivie nods in agreement.

We spend the rest of the flight in relative quiet. We check weapons for the fifth time, just in case. With a face made of stone, Ivie tucks her sidearm into the holster at the small of her back after checking the magazine.

She's not shaky. She's not upset.

She's on a mission.

I glance at Curt and see him nod. He's thinking the same thing I am. She needs this. No matter how much I want to protect her from it, to shelter her, she needs it.

And we'll be here for her through it.

Shortly after landing in Dallas, we climb into a large, black SUV, and Rocco drives us to a suburb, while a guard drives my father and Igor to another location.

They didn't tell us where they were going, just that they had someone to pay a visit to.

I hope they're not going to see the Dallas syndicate without us. I know that our fathers are powerful men, but they shouldn't go in alone. This isn't the time.

But I'm not the boss. They are. And what they say

goes. I have to block that out, secure in the knowledge that they're not currently in danger, and focus entirely on Ivie and the mission ahead.

"That's his," Rocco says, pointing to a small house as we drive past. The curtains are drawn in the front, but not the sides. The blue paint is peeling as if the person living there hasn't had the money or inclination to keep it painted.

"Bastard is living better than he ever did when I was a kid," Ivie mutters. "Why aren't you stopping?"

"Because we need to make sure nothing is going on," I reply and take her hand in mine. To my relief, she doesn't pull away. "Rocco will circle the block, just to be sure that everything is calm, and then we'll park a few houses down so we don't draw attention."

"Right." She blows out a breath. "Sorry, I'm impatient. And I'm so damn *mad.*"

"Impatience will get you killed," Curt says from behind her. "Slow your body down, Ivie. Take a deep breath, then another. Calm your mind. If you rush, if you let your anger lead, you'll fail."

"I won't fail," she vows softly and follows Curt's orders by taking a deep breath.

When we've parked several houses down from Pavlov, I reach for the door handle, but Ivie stops me.

"I'm going in alone."

"Ivie—"

"I know you want to protect me." She takes my hand and gazes up at me with those intense blue eyes.

"I know that. It's who you are, Shane, and I appreciate you so much. I appreciate everything you've done for me. But like I said earlier, I'm no damsel in distress here. *You* made sure of that. I've been training for this for weeks, and I didn't even realize it. I need time with him. I have things to say."

"You have fifteen minutes," I reply reluctantly. "And then we're coming in. This isn't up for negotiation."

"I'd take that offer," Carmine says. "It's the best you'll get from us."

"Okay, I'll see you soon." She nods once and then, without hesitation, steps from the vehicle, looks both ways, and crosses the street. She walks up the sidewalk and then up the steps to the front porch.

She doesn't bother knocking, just walks right inside. My gut twists.

"Jesus." I pull my hand down my face in frustration. "I never would have thought I'd let her do this."

"She needs it," Curt says. "And I know how she feels."

After everything Curt's been through, he would understand perfectly.

"Yeah, well, she's not a trained operative."

"But she's trained with her weapon and hand-to-hand. Her father is an old man now. She can protect herself."

"It's different when it's blood," Nadia says, her voice hollow as she stares at the door Ivie just walked through.

Nadia killed her brother earlier this year after discovering he was behind a plot to double-cross his family.

I can't imagine the bad moments she's had since then, even knowing that what she did was the right thing.

Carmine wraps his arm around her shoulders and whispers something in her ear.

We're quiet for a long moment, and then Rocco says quietly, "Is the hair standing up on anyone else's neck?"

"Something isn't right," Carmine agrees.

The air is too still.

It's too quiet.

"Let's go." I pull my weapon from its holster. "Nadia and Carmine, take the right side of the house. Curt and I will take the left. Rocco—"

"I'm going *up*," my brother says with a hard voice.

We can't see the roof of the house from here. I don't know how Rocco intends to do what he has planned, but he's more than capable.

With weapons drawn, we move silently across the street to the house. My heart is pounding harder than it ever has on any other mission. I'm usually like stone, perfectly calm. But I've never faced the possibility of losing someone I love on a mission before. This is new territory.

I don't plan to ever repeat it.

I just keep silently berating myself for letting her go

in alone. I should be in there with her. I should be by her side.

But then Curt's words come into my head. If I let the frustration, the *fear*, take over, I'll lose. I have to remain focused and steady. For her sake and that of everyone here.

We're a team, and we have a fucking job to do.

As soon as Curt and I walk around the house's left corner, we come face-to-face with two armed men dressed in black.

We silently neutralize them and keep walking, leaving the bodies where they fell.

How did we not see them from the front? Were they hiding?

What the hell is happening here?

We slip around the corner to the back yard in time to see Carmine and Nadia kill two men. Curt and I take care of two more headed their way.

"Six?" I ask.

"Eight," Carmine replies.

"Twelve," Rocco says as he jumps down from above.

"Jesus," I whisper and immediately move to the back door.

"There are men inside," Carmine says grimly. "I counted two in the kitchen. I saw three people in the living room, but that doesn't mean there aren't more."

"There's no one upstairs," Rocco adds. "It's clear."

We kill two more in the kitchen.

Fourteen men.

I motion for the others to stop and be silent, and I quickly look around the corner where I hear a man speaking rapidly in a foreign language.

There is no one else in the house that I can see. Just Ivie, her father, and the other man yelling at them.

"Bulgarian," Nadia whispers in my ear.

I turn to look at the others and point to myself.

I go in first.

They nod once.

But when I turn back around, all hell has already broken loose.

CHAPTER 19

~IVIE~

*O*nce across the street from Shane and the others, I snap my spine straight and clear my throat.

No hesitation. No nerves.

This is a long time coming, and I'm going to take advantage of it. It's an opportunity I never thought to get. Just hours ago, I was thinking that I'd never have my mama with me to fluff my dress and giggle with my friends before I got married.

And it's *his* fault.

I get to make him pay.

But before I do, I have a lot to say to the man I thought was dead. I won't waste the moment.

I climb the small house's rickety steps. He lives in a beautiful neighborhood, but his home is starting to crumble. It doesn't surprise me. I wonder if the neighbors are pissed that he's bringing their property values down.

Without knocking, I turn the doorknob, surprised to find it unlocked. I walk right in.

The space smells of him—tobacco and stale onions. I would never forget that smell. The air carries a light haze from cigarettes. There's a TV on upstairs.

The furniture is old and has holes in the cushions. A photo of my mother on the wall has me seeing red.

How *dare* he?

"Hello?"

The man who sired me walks into the living room and stops cold, staring at me with surprised eyes.

"Have a seat," I tell him with a hard voice.

"Laryssa."

"Does not exist," I reply calmly. "Sit the fuck down, Pavlov."

His face turns red, and his eyes narrow. "You will not speak to me like that."

"Oh, I'm gonna speak to you any way I see fit, you piece of trash. If you don't want to sit, that's fine. You can hear me just fine while standing."

"How did you find me?"

"It doesn't matter. I am going to do the talking, and I want the damn *truth*. Why did you kill my mother?"

He glances toward the photo on the wall.

"No, don't you dare look at her. Why did you kill her? Cut her throat?"

"Because I was given an order to," he says simply.

I stare at him, unblinking. This man that scared me so badly as a child, who hurt me on a whim, looks so old and frail now. I'm as tall as he is. His face is wrinkled, his eyes dull. He's lost most of his dark hair.

He's a shell of the man he once was.

"You were supposed to die," he continues. His voice still carries the thick Bulgarian accent from my youth. "I spared you."

"So I could do your dirty work." I shake my head and prop my hands on my hips. "So I could steal and deliver shit that you didn't want to be caught with. You spared me so gross, old men could ogle me—a *child*—and give you what you wanted."

"And it worked. We were a good team, you and me, Laryssa."

"I said Laryssa doesn't fucking exist. I killed her and created someone new. Someone who doesn't carry your name, who has nothing at all to do with you. And I've done a damn good job of making a nice life for myself."

"In the mafia," he says with a nasty sneer. "How appropriate."

"So you knew where I was, after all. And you never came after me."

"You started to have a mouth on you. I knew that you didn't always deliver what I sent you to do, and that no matter how much I punished you, you wouldn't fall in line. Just like your mother. It angered me when you ran away, but I had other problems to see to.

Worrying about where you ended up was not a priority."

I wanted the truth, and he was giving it to me.

There was a time when his words would have hurt me.

But not now.

"You're a worthless piece of garbage," I inform him.

"The apple doesn't fall far from the tree, Laryssa."

I snarl, but then Igor's words come back to me. *Family isn't always blood.*

"I was never your daughter in any way that mattered. I was a tool. And I got out. I'm *nothing* like you."

"Aren't you? Are you telling me then that you're not here to kill me?"

"Oh, I'm going to kill you," I agree. "But not because I'm the same as you. No, I'm going to kill you because you slit my mother's throat and left me motherless."

"She was nothing."

"Is that why you still have her photo hanging on your wall? Because she was nothing?"

He narrows his eyes, and his hands fist at his sides.

"I did not realize you'd let your daughter speak to you in such a disrespectful way."

We turn as a man walks into the room from what must be the kitchen, gun in hand. He's tall and lean with round, wire-rimmed glasses. He looks like Doc from *Back to the Future.*

And his accent is the same as my father's.

"Both of you, sit," he instructs us, pointing to the two chairs facing an empty television. I eye him, considering whether I can fight him for the gun, but he steps forward. "I said, sit."

Pavlov sits, glaring at the man, and I sit next to him.

"I am Elian Pavlov."

I scowl. "Pavlov?"

"That's right. I'm your father's brother. Your uncle. We're just a big, happy family."

"I'll break out the photo albums. Oh, wait, we don't have any. Because we aren't a family."

Elian doesn't smile. "Your father's past transgressions when he was still living in our homeland have caught up with him."

"The transgressions from after he left Bulgaria have caught up with him, too."

Suddenly, Elian starts speaking rapidly in Bulgarian and pacing the room as if a switch was flipped and something I said—or didn't say—set off his temper.

"What are you saying?"

He doesn't reply, just keeps going, pointing at me and then my father.

"What the fuck are you saying? I don't speak Bulgarian!"

He stops and stares at Ivan. "You did not teach her?"

"He taught me how to be a son of a bitch, and that about covers it."

"He is saying—" my father begins, but I cut him off by holding up my hand.

"No. I've said all I need to say to you, and I don't want to hear another word from your lying mouth. You,"—I point to my uncle—"you talk."

He pushes his face close to mine. "You may speak to your father like that, but I won't allow it."

I raise an eyebrow. "I don't fucking *know* you. And, frankly, I don't care who you are."

I have no idea where this bravado is coming from, aside from the fact that I'm damn sick and tired of the men in my family being assholes.

Elian backhands me with the butt of his sidearm, making me see stars.

"You will speak with respect, the way a woman should."

I glare at him.

My father shifts next to me.

And then I look at them, back and forth, as the situation starts to make sense.

"Have you been here this whole time?" I ask Elian.

"Of course."

"You followed us."

He smiles thinly. "You're smarter than you look."

"There's a mole." I shake my head. "There's a mole in the Martinellis' organization."

"I've been watching you for a long time, Laryssa," Elian says and then laughs. "I mean...Ivie. We finally had you in our grasp in New York, but you managed to wiggle your way out of that."

"You were behind the kidnapping."

"No," my father says as he stands next to his brother. "I was."

My mouth drops open. I stare at the two men and then narrow my eyes as pieces start to click into place. "Are you *twins*?"

"Triplets, actually," Elian says. "Our brother was hanged just over twelve years ago."

I blink rapidly as the last of the puzzle fits together. "You killed your brother to hide your death, and then you let the Sergis hide you?"

"We used their money," my father says. "Let them think they were the ones I was funneling information to. Let them believe they were in charge."

"They were not," Elian adds.

"What do I have to do with any of this?"

"You took the drive," Ivan says with the shake of his head. "When you ran away, you took the information with you."

"For fuck's sake." I sigh and shake my head slowly. "Something I didn't even remember I had until two weeks ago is the reason you've wanted me dead?"

"Not dead, necessarily," Elian says. "Just found. All this time, if you'd done what you were instructed to do in the first place, you could have gone on living your life, none the wiser. But you didn't. Where is it?"

"I don't know."

"Liar," Ivan says and reaches for me, but I duck out of his grasp and move quickly away. "Where is it?"

"I certainly don't have it on me," I reply and evade him again.

Both Elian and Ivan start speaking in rapid Bulgarian, and I can't understand them again.

Why didn't I stay brushed up on the language?

"Stop moving."

I look at Elian, his words spoken in English, and stare down the barrel of his weapon.

Before he can pull the trigger, a knife appears at this throat and slices deep, spattering blood everywhere.

"Jesus."

My father is holding the knife and staring at me with hollow, dead eyes.

Shane bursts into the room, his weapon drawn, but I shake my head.

This is *my* fight.

"Tell me where the drive is, Laryssa."

"I told you." I stomp his foot, ram my knee into his crotch, and grab the knife from his hand, then drive it right into his heart. As his mouth gapes, and his eyes bulge, I lean into him. "My name is *Ivie*."

As he gurgles, I pull out the knife and rest the blade against his throat.

"And this is for my mama."

Without hesitation, I slice from left to right and let him fall, next to his brother.

The blood is revolting. It covers *everything*. Me, the floor, the walls, and the furniture.

But I ignore it and walk to the wall to pluck the

photo of my mother from the nail. I use my sleeve to wipe blood spatter from the glass.

"I'm taking you with me." I kiss her and then turn to Shane. "Get me the hell out of here."

"On it, baby." He nods to the others, who flank me, and helps me out of the house and to the vehicle.

"I'm calling in cleanup," Carmine says as we get settled in the vehicle, and he takes out his phone.

Rafe fires up the car, and we pull away from the curb and head back the way we came.

"Plane's ready," Rafe says.

"There were two of him," Shane says, turning to me.

"His brother." I tell them everything that happened after I walked into the house. "He had *two* brothers that I didn't even know about."

"None of us did," Shane says. "It didn't come up in the research."

"They framed the Sergis," Nadia says in surprise. "My God, who the fuck are they?"

"Bulgarian operatives," Curt says, getting all our attention. "I recognized Elian's name. But Pavlov is a common Bulgarian name, so I didn't link him with Ivan. I've never seen a photo of him. He was a slimy, sneaky son of a bitch. He was on every hit list in the fucking world."

"Well, he was hit." My hands have started to shake. "By his own brother."

"Are you hurt?" Shane asks me. "Tell me all this blood is theirs."

"It's theirs." I swallow hard and feel sick to my stomach. *Oh God, do not get sick here. Hold on.* "I need a shower."

"We have one on the plane," Rafe says as he changes lanes. "I'll have you there in ten minutes."

It takes eight.

Shane helps me up the stairs where Igor and Carlo are waiting for us.

"Oh, little one," Igor says, but I hold up my hand.

"Not yet." I look up at him with pleading eyes. "I need to clean up and gather myself."

"Of course." Carlo points to the back of the plane. "Everything you need is back there, Ivie. Make yourself at home."

"I'm coming with you," Shane says, and I don't argue. I *need* him now—more than I ever have before.

I manage to hold myself together while he starts the shower and helps me out of my ruined clothes.

"There isn't enough room in there for both of us," he says grimly.

"I'm shocked we're in a plane," I say. "It's huge."

"There's soap, shampoo, and anything else you need." He opens the glass door for me, but before I can step inside, he cups my face in his hands and kisses me gently. "Take your time, love. We won't take off until you're ready."

"Thank you." It's a whisper. I climb into the shower and let the hot water beat on me, just soaking in the warmth.

I'm so cold. I can't stop shaking.

Maybe this is shock.

Finally, I reach for the soap and start washing up. My hair is next. When I'm as clean as I can get, and as warm as I'm *going* to get for now, I open the shower door.

Shane is waiting with a big, fluffy towel.

"Come here."

I step out to him, and he wraps me in that terrycloth and pulls me to him. I lose control and cling to him as I start sobbing. I've always thought that people who wail when they cry are just dramatic, but I get it now as I bawl against the strongest man I've ever met.

The man I love with all my heart and soul.

And grieve once more for the mother I loved so much, and the father I hated with everything in me.

When I've quieted to soft hiccups, Shane finishes drying me and wraps me in a white robe, then leads me out of the bathroom and into the bedroom with a queen-sized bed.

He pushes a button and speaks into a microphone.

"She's out of the shower, and we're safe in the bedroom. You're cleared for takeoff."

Shane pulls back the crisp, white linens, and we lie down, tangled in each other, just clinging to one another as we hear the engines come to life and feel the plane start making its way down the runway.

When we're airborne, and my tears have stopped flowing, Shane turns my chin his way.

"I'm so proud of you, sweetheart."

My chin wobbles, but I lick my lips and rub his nose with mine. "I wasn't scared. I was just…mad. And when I killed him, I wasn't sorry."

"Yeah. I get that."

"Does that make me an evil person?" I wonder aloud. "Does it make me like *him* that I was able to end his life with no remorse?"

"No." His voice is firm as he urges me to look him in the eyes. "You're not evil, Ivie, you're human. It's over now. He's gone, and he can't hurt you ever again. We'll do some more digging to make sure that it ends with Ivan and Elian. I suspect it does, but we'll cross every *t* and dot every *i*, just to be sure."

I nod and blow out a breath. "It's over."

"Yes."

My breath hitches. "Curt can go home, where he's happiest."

His lips twitch. "I'm so happy to hear that you're worried about Curt."

"What will you do?" I ask.

Shane's eyes sober. His hand cups my cheek again, and just when I think he's going to kiss me, he says, "I love you, Ivie. I love you more than I ever thought I could love someone. You've wound your way inside me, and I can't let you go.

"So, to answer your question, I'm going to talk to

the people I work for and set new parameters there. Because I refuse to ever leave you alone. I will *not* put myself into a position that might mean I never come home to you."

A tear falls down my cheek, but it's not because of my father. It's from the hope that's just set up residence in my belly.

"I love you, too."

"Good." He grins and kisses me lightly but then pulls back again. "I'm glad to hear that, sweetheart because I'd like to ask you a serious question now. I'd get on one knee, but this feels a little more intimate, and pretty much perfect for us since we haven't done anything the traditional way since the day I met you."

I bite my lip, waiting.

"Marry me, Ivie. Make me the luckiest man in the world. I know that my family is a lot to take on, and as crazy as they are, they will love and protect you until the day they die. You will never want for anything. You'll never wonder for even one moment how much I love you, how devoted I am to you. Be my wife."

"That sounded more like a command than a question."

His lips twitch. "Well, I'm used to giving orders, so..."

I laugh and wrap my arms around him. "Yes, Shane Martinelli. I'll be your wife. Under one condition."

"What's that?"

"You give me babies. I want lots of children. I might

not come from the best of parents, but I know I'll be a good mom."

A slow smile spreads over his gorgeous face. "I'm on board with that. In fact—" He pushes the robe open and slides a talented hand inside. "Why don't we get a head start on that?"

"You'll get no argument from me."

"That's a first."

EPILOGUE

~ANNIKA~

One Month Later...

"*I*t is my honor to introduce you to Mr. and Mrs. Martinelli!"

We all stand and clap as Nadia and Carmine walk into the ballroom of the Martinelli family home just outside of Seattle. She's changed into the sexier gown she bought, just for the reception.

Leave it to my cousin Nadia to be more than a little *extra* on her wedding day.

But I wouldn't have her any other way.

The weather held beautifully for the ceremony out by the pond. There were even swans swimming gracefully across the still water as Ivie and I stood by Nadia's side and watched with pride as our best friend promised to join her life with Carmine's.

I don't think there was a dry eye in the audience. Even Igor, my uncle, wiped a tear from his eye as he gave his daughter away.

The house is packed with at least three hundred guests, and likely close to that many vendors, here to make sure that Nadia's day goes off without a hitch.

And I'd say, so far, it's been absolutely perfect.

"Come dance with me."

I glance up at Rafe and feel my heart pick up speed, the way it always does when he's near. I've loved this man since I was nineteen.

And he loves me.

But we can't be together.

"Come on," he says, urging me to follow him to the floor. "It's just a dance, Annika. I'm not asking you to marry me or anything."

I frown at him but melt against him when he wraps those strong arms around me and guides me into a sweet, slow dance.

I've gotten good at saying "*no*" to Rafe.

But it feels so wonderful when I give in and say, "Yes."

I rest my cheek against his muscled chest and close my eyes, letting the music fill me. And for this moment, I almost forget that I'm damaged goods and that if Rafe ever found out what my secrets are, he'd stop asking me to let him in.

To give him a chance.

To give *us* a chance.

They all think that the worst part of me died with my husband.

But they're wrong.

When the song ends, a fast one starts, and Nadia makes me stay on the floor with her as we jam out to music from when we were young and would dance our asses off in her bedroom.

When I can barely feel my feet anymore, I wave them off and make my way to the table to change my shoes into flats—I'm a smart woman who brings appropriate footwear when I know dancing will be involved—and take a sip of water.

"Oh, honey, you look absolutely gorgeous today," Katya, Nadia's mom, says as she leans in to kiss my cheek. "Don't you think everything came together nicely?"

Katya is a typical mother, even though she's married to a billionaire and can have anything she wants with the snap of her fingers. She just wants her daughter's special day to be perfect. And she's been fretting for days.

"It's so lovely," I assure her. "You were right to go with the lilacs outside. They smelled heavenly, and added just the right pop of color."

"Oh, I'm so happy to hear you say that," she says with a whoosh of relieved breath. "I was worried that someone would be allergic. That's why we went with simple roses in here, just in case."

"You never miss a thing, Aunt Katya." I kiss her cheek. "Are you going to dance with Uncle Igor?"

She glances over to where her husband is smoking cigars with Carlo and the Sergi boss. "He'll save some dances for me. In the meantime, I'm going to let him tell tall tales with his friends and drink some whiskey."

Aunt Katya winks at me.

"The secret to being married to a man like Igor is to let him think he's always in charge, while having the backbone to steer him where he needs to go." She glances over, and I follow her gaze. She's looking at Rafe. "You remember that, my love."

"Oh, I don't think—"

"It's just a suggestion," she interrupts and then kisses me on the cheek before rushing over to chat with a table full of guests.

Everyone thinks I should be with Rafe. Even *Rafe* is convinced I should be with him.

But they're wrong.

I sigh and sit at my table, reaching for the bag beneath the tablecloth so I can change my shoes when a waiter taps my shoulder.

"Miss Annika?"

"Yes?"

"This was just delivered for you. They said it was urgent, so I brought it right over."

"Oh?" I frown at the manila envelope and nod at the young man. "Thank you."

He nods and hurries away. I glance around to make sure no one is looking over my shoulder and open the envelope.

There's a note on top.

If you do not meet our demands, we will send these to the press. Your family will be ruined. You will be ruined.

We will be in touch.

I flip the note to the back and feel my blood run cold as I stare down at the first photograph.

It's from another lifetime. When the man I married made me do things that I hated, that I was uncomfortable with. Things I'm not proud of.

My nakedness is on full display in the photo. And the next one. The third shows me doing things I'd never even *think* of doing again.

Suddenly, I feel a strong hand on my shoulder and look up into Rafe's hot blue eyes.

"What the fuck is that?"

TURN the page for a sneak peek at the final installment in the With Me In Seattle MAFIA series, Off the Record:

OFF THE RECORD

A WITH ME IN SEATTLE MAFIA NOVEL

Off the Record
A With Me In Seattle MAFIA Novel
By

Kristen Proby

PROLOGUE

~ANNIKA~

*R*afe Martinelli. Also known as the love of my life. The man of my dreams. My one and only. I know, I'm only twenty, and my cousin Nadia would tell me that it's completely ridiculous to think that I could meet my soul mate in college when I should be out sowing my wild oats—whatever in the world that means.

I love Nadia. She's my closest friend, as well as my cousin, and she's one of a very select few who knows what it's like to live in this crazy family of ours. My roommate, Ivie, knows.

And Rafe.

Because while my uncle is the boss of one of the most prominent crime families in the country, Rafe's father is the boss of *the* biggest family on the west coast.

And our families don't like each other.

Which means that everything Rafe and I are to each other, everything we've done, and what we're about to do tonight is a secret.

Because if our families found out, we'd be in big trouble.

"Class dismissed."

I sigh in relief when my biology professor gives us the okay to leave. I gather my books and papers and rush out of the lab toward my car.

Ivie and I live in an apartment just on the edge of campus. My uncle is kind enough to pay for it. Lord knows, neither Ivie nor I could pay for it ourselves.

I know I'm a lucky girl.

My date with Rafe is in an hour. Which means, I have to take a shower and get ready to go fast because Rafe is never late.

It's just one of the million reasons I love him so much.

"Hi, friend," I announce as I rush past Ivie to my bedroom. "Can't talk. Gotta hurry."

"I'll follow you," she says and leans her shoulder against the door of my bedroom as I strip naked and make a beeline for the bathroom. "What lit a fire under your butt?"

"Date."

"With Rafe?"

"It'd better be with Rafe. He'd be pretty mad if it was with someone else."

Ivie smirks as I start the shower and throw my hair

up under a shower cap. She's the only one who knows about Rafe and me. I *had* to tell her. She lives here, and I spend a lot of time with him.

"Tonight's the night," I inform her.

"Of what? Is there a new movie out?"

"No, it's *the* night."

She flings the shower curtain back and stares at me with wide, blue eyes. "You're going to *do it*?"

"Yep." I smile and shave one armpit. "I've been on the pill for a month, so we're covered there. I mean, we've literally done *everything* else. It's borderline torture. I'm so ready. He does things to me that I didn't even know were possible. The way I feel when he looks at me, let alone what happens to my skin, to my stomach when he touches me... I'm telling you, Ivie, it's incredible."

"I'm totally jealous." She pulls the curtain shut again, but I can hear her organizing things on the countertop. "Also, you're stupidly hot together. Like, you could be a celebrity couple, you're so pretty. It's like Brangelina."

I lather up one leg but pull the curtain aside so I can grin at my best friend. "You're so sweet. Thank you."

"I think you should tell your parents."

"No." I get to work shaving and shake my head, even though she can't see me. "No way. Uncle Igor would throw a fit, and I'd be in big trouble. I don't even want to think about what the punishment for this would be. And for Rafe, it would be worse. So, no. It's our secret."

243

"But what happens after this, Annika? I know it's exciting now, but you won't be in college forever. What then? Are you going to get married in secret and have secret babies?"

Tears want to threaten, but I swallow them and rinse my legs.

"Stop it. Tonight is going to be special, and I'm not going to think about the future and ruin it. It'll all work out. All I can do is live day to day."

I wrap the towel around me and immediately reach for my makeup bag.

"I don't agree with you, but I hope tonight is everything you want it to be." She pats me on the shoulder and leaves the bathroom, and I stare at my reflection.

"Everything's going to be just fine."

"Are you okay?"

"You've asked me that about six times." I smile at Rafe as he tucks a loose strand of hair behind my ear. The truth is, I'm sore, and it hurt way more than I thought it would, and was over pretty fast, too. But I've also never felt more connected to a person in my life as I do right now, lying in Rafe's giant bed.

"Are *you* okay?" I ask him and drag my fingertip down his nose. Rafe is a handsome man. He's tall and broad, and I know he works out almost every day. The efforts show. He has muscles on top of muscles and tanned skin. I could lick every inch of him.

And have.

"I don't think I've ever been better." His smile is soft, lazy, and a little proud. "You're amazing, babe."

I grin and rest my head on his shoulder. When I draw circles on his chest, he clasps my hand in his, kisses it, then holds it against his heart.

"I wish we could just stay right here, forever," I whisper.

"Me, too."

"What do you think will happen?"

He sighs. He knows exactly what I'm talking about.

"I don't mean to ruin this night," I rush on. "Forget I said anything."

"You didn't ruin anything," he assures me and kisses my forehead. "And the honest answer is, I don't know."

"We're meant to be together," I continue. "I mean, how else do you explain that we randomly chose the same college? And on the east coast, no less? This isn't a fluke. It's destiny. Maybe we can convince our families of that. Eventually."

"Maybe." He kisses my forehead again. "Eventually."

Two years later...

I've been summoned to my uncle's office. I don't

quite know what to make of that, given that it's never happened before.

I smile at his assistant, who nods and says, "You can go on in, Annika."

"Thanks."

I push through the milky glass doors and am surprised to see not only Uncle Igor but also my father.

"Close the door, please," Uncle Igor says. He's sitting behind his enormous desk, looking more powerful than any man I've ever seen.

But he's never frightened me. He's always been loving and generous with me.

"Is something wrong?" I ask as I sit in the chair across from my uncle, next to my father.

"No. Actually, we have some good news for you. But first, I want to congratulate you on doing so well in college, my little firefly." Uncle Igor smiles proudly. "You finished your bachelors in just three years, and you're on track to finish medical school in only two years."

"That's right. And I want to thank *you* for the opportunity. I know it's not inexpensive, and I appreciate everything the family has done for me."

"I know you do. You're a good girl, Annika." Uncle Igor and my father share a look. "I wanted to let you know that you'll be moving to Denver for your residency."

I frown and shake my head. "I don't understand."

"You'll be switching schools in the fall. You'll complete your residency in Denver."

What about Rafe?

"Why? I'm doing well here, and I like this college. I have friends here."

"I know." He folds his hands on his desk. "And a boyfriend, eh?"

I blink rapidly. I *hate* lying to my family. "No, of course, not."

He tosses several photos on the desk in front of me, and I swallow hard when I see images of Rafe and me, walking hand-in-hand on campus, laughing while seated at our favorite restaurant, and kissing on a bridge where we like to take walks.

"You've never been a liar before, firefly."

I feel my father shift next to me, and tears immediately threaten.

"I don't like lying now," I confess and swallow hard.

"You know that the Martinellis are off-limits."

I clasp my hands tightly in my lap.

"Look at me," he says, but his voice is gentle, and his eyes hold compassion when I meet his. "You fancy yourself in love, do you?"

"Yes."

He nods and turns to look out the windows.

"He was sent here to follow you."

I blink, certain I've heard him wrong.

"They're keeping an eye on you and trying to get

247

information. The fact that they'd stoop so low and use my innocent niece as a pawn is unforgivable."

"No, that's not what's happening. Rafe was surprised to see me. We didn't know we were attending the same college."

"Annika," Papa says beside me and reaches for my hand. "You know this is not possible. It's forbidden."

A tear drops onto my cheek. "I didn't mean to fall in love with him any more than I can be to blame for his family tree."

"You're smarter than this," Uncle Igor says. "And I'm ending it. Now. Your last day of class is Friday. You'll be packed up and moved by Saturday afternoon. I've already arranged for the movers. This is not up for discussion."

My world is crumbling out from under me.

"What about Ivie?"

"She'll go with you. I know she's your closest friend and your confidante. I'm not a monster."

I have to try. I have to fight for what Rafe and I have. "Please, Uncle Igor. If you could just listen. If you could maybe talk to Rafe..."

"I am not at fault here," he replies, his voice hard now. "You know what it means to be a part of this family. You *know* that the Martinellis are off-limits. You need to remember your place and be grateful that simply changing schools is your punishment for defying me."

He's all boss now. I know better than to talk back.

So, I simply nod.

"Yes, sir."

"Good. End it today. I have an apartment waiting for you and Ivie in Denver. It's in a nice part of town and is newer than the place you have here."

"Thank you." It's a whisper.

When they dismiss me, I walk on numb legs out of the office building and stand on the sidewalk in the sunshine.

My God, how will I tell him?

CHAPTER 1

~RAFE~

Present Day

"They *met* with him?" I demand. I shove my hands into the pockets of my tux and work at keeping my face bland.

We're at a wedding, for Christ's sake.

"Pop confirmed it last night," Carmine says, rocking back on his heels. "I meant to pull you both in and tell you, but things got crazy."

"It was the night before your wedding," Shane reminds him. "Of course, it's crazy. What in the hell were they thinking, going in there alone? They're too old for that shit."

I share a look with my brothers, and then we all chuckle.

"They may be older," I reply, speaking of our father and Carmine's new father-in-law, Igor Tarenkov—

they're both bosses of two of the strongest crime families in the world, "but they're not weak. They're also smart. If they went in to talk to those in Carlito's office without us, they knew what they were doing."

"Yeah, well," Carmine says, "I wish they'd let us in on it."

"This isn't the time or place," Shane says and claps a hand on our eldest brother's shoulder. "We're here to celebrate. Go dance with your bride. I'm going to find my smokin' hot fiancée and take her for a spin around the dance floor myself. Did you see how hot she looks today?"

Carmine and I smile as Shane hurries off to find Ivie.

"She's good for him," I say, watching as our brother takes Ivie's hand, kisses it, and then pulls her onto the dance floor. "She makes him happy."

"She does." Carmine nods and then glances to our left, motioning with his head. "She seems to frustrate you."

I follow his gaze and sigh when my eyes land on Annika. My gut churns, the way it always does whenever I see the woman I've loved for almost a decade.

"She does more than that," I murmur and sip my champagne. "I want to kiss the fuck out of her and take her over my damn knee."

Carmine laughs and taps his glass to mine. "That's a woman for you. I think I'll follow our brother's lead and go find my wife."

His grin flashes over his face.

"My wife."

"You went and chained yourself to a dame for the rest of your life."

"Hell, yes. And I'd do it again in a heartbeat if it meant I could marry Nadia all over again."

"I guess you're allowed to be sappy on your wedding day. Go find your bride and dance inappropriately for a while."

"My pleasure."

Carmine saunters across the room, his eyes set on Nadia. She's a beautiful bride, and her eyes light up when she turns to see Carmine approaching.

They're both a couple of saps.

I guess I would be, too. I turn to look at Annika once more and sigh. She's as stunning as ever, with her long, blond hair falling around her in loose curls. Her makeup is flawless and more glammed-up for the occasion. The dress she's in showcases every curve to perfection, and my fingers ache with my desire to touch her.

Hell, it's not just my fingers that ache.

But I've gotten good at admiring her from afar. Keeping my distance.

Giving her space.

But my patience is running thin.

Her piece-of-shit husband has been dead for months. Nothing's standing in our way now.

Nothing except her stubbornness.

I set my empty glass on a tray and walk to where Annika is sitting, alone. She's holding an envelope, and I watch as she tears it open, quickly pages through the contents, and then runs a shaking hand through that silky hair.

I'm not at all ashamed that I look over her shoulder.

I almost wish I hadn't.

The image in her hands has my blood running cold.

"What the fuck is that?"

She jumps, puts the photo face-down on the table, and turns to me. "Oh, you startled me. It's nothing."

"I'll put up with a lot of things from you, Annika, but lying isn't one of them." I lean down, leveling my gaze with hers. "What is that?"

She swallows hard, glances down, and shoves everything back into the envelope. "Not now. Not here. It's Nadia's special day, and I won't ruin it with this. Especially not with this."

She turns embarrassed eyes up to me.

"Annika."

"Let's dance." She shoves the envelope into a bag under the table, takes my hand, and tries to pull me onto the dance floor.

But I outweigh her by at least a hundred pounds and stand my ground.

She looks up at me, sighs, then retrieves the envelope and leads me out of my grandmother's ballroom and to a nearby empty room.

"I don't want this to go *anywhere* but this room for

254

today," she says, her voice strong, her tone saying it isn't open for discussion. "It's my best friend—my *cousin's* special day. Got it?"

I can't promise her that. But I nod. "I'll do everything I can not to ruin the day."

She blows out a breath and pulls a note out of the envelope, passing it to me.

If you do not meet our demands, we will send these to the press. Your family will be ruined. You *will be ruined.*

We will be in touch.

I scowl and look up at Annika. "Who the fuck sent this?"

"You know as much as I do." She shifts her feet.

"Show me the rest."

"No." She shakes her head quickly. "These are private photos, and I don't want you to see them. It's humiliating. You saw the last one."

What I thought I saw was Annika, naked, spread-eagle and tied to a bed with a group of men standing around her.

And by the look on her face, I'd say my memory isn't wrong.

I want to fucking *kill* someone.

I was her first. I knew everything about her, once upon a time.

Is this who she is now?

"I don't want to talk about it."

No. By the look on her face, I'd say that's not who she is. I have so many fucking questions.

"Here you are," Nadia says as she walks into the room, a bright smile on her face. "I thought I saw you leave. We're about to cut the cake."

The new bride stops talking and glances back and forth between us.

"What's wrong? Are you arguing again?"

"No." Annika pastes on a smile. "Of course, not. We were just talking."

"She needs to know."

The color leaves Annika's face, and Nadia turns to me, all badass now. "What the fuck is going on?"

Carmine walks in behind her and cocks a brow.

I pass them the note as Annika curses and paces away to look out the window.

"Who is this from?" Nadia asks, but Annika doesn't turn back from the window.

"We don't know," I reply softly. "There are photos, as well."

"Let me see," Nadia demands.

"No," Annika says, shaking her head. "Let's just forget this and go back to the party. We're ruining your day."

"Someone is *threatening* you," Carmine says, his voice much gentler than the look in his eyes. "Let us have the information, and if we can't handle it today, we'll tuck it away and push it aside until tomorrow."

Annika turns to him, her bottom lip trembling.

I want to pull her into my arms and assure her that everything will be okay.

But I can't.

She wouldn't welcome it, and I don't know that everything *will* be okay. I can't lie to her.

"Photos." She passes them to Nadia. "Do *not* show those to Carmine."

Nadia frowns, looks at the images, and then gasps. "*Annika.*"

"What are you guys doing in here?" Ivie asks as she and Shane walk in.

"Close and lock that door," I say to Shane, who frowns but does as I ask.

I quickly fill them in on what we know, which isn't much, and Nadia shows Ivie the photos.

"Jesus, Annika," Ivie breathes. "What in the ever-loving hell is this?"

Annika shakes her head, fights tears, and I go to her and take her hand, giving it a firm squeeze as I smile down at her.

"We're your friends and your family. You're safe here, honey."

She takes a deep breath.

"I really wish we didn't have to have this conversation right now—or ever." She licks her lips. "For now, let's just say that Richard was a son of a bitch. And after we got married, he turned into someone I didn't know. He had certain...*preferences*. If I denied him, he punished me, but also if I *agreed*—so to speak. Obviously, someone took photos, and they're trying to make a buck or two off of it. No biggie. I can afford to pay them to go away."

"Fuck that."

"No way."

"Absolutely, not."

Annika stares at all of us as we fume around her.

"You pay them this time, and they'll just come back for more," I inform her. "Besides, it doesn't say they want money. It doesn't specify the demands. I assume they'll be in touch again."

"I'll handle it." Her chin comes up, and she squares her shoulders. "I. Will. Handle. It. Now, I want all of you to go back to the party. Me, too, actually. I need a stiff drink."

"We're sticking close," I insist.

"Of course, you are. You're my people. Now, let's go have cake and champagne and get damn good and drunk in celebration."

We all exchange looks but nod and follow Annika back to the ballroom.

Carmine, Shane, and I hang back a bit as Ivie and Nadia flank Annika as they walk down the hall.

"We meet in the office at oh-nine-hundred," Carmine says. "All six of us. We'll figure this out."

"Copy that," I agree.

~

"OH, MY GOD, I'M HUNGOVER." Ivie walks into the office, makes a beeline for the coffee and donuts set up on the credenza, and sinks into a brown leather chair, her eyes closed. "Sugar will help."

"I feel great," Nadia says as she pours herself some coffee. "Must have been all that married sex we had all night long."

Carmine winks at his bride and takes a sip of his own coffee as Shane and Annika walk through the door.

"I found this one in the kitchen, sulking over a bowl of Cocoa Puffs."

She's still carrying the bowl.

"I'm not sulking."

"Well, you weren't smiling," Shane says and sits on the arm of Ivie's chair. "Hey, baby."

"Hey. I'm consuming all the sugar to help fight this hangover. I know better than to get drunk on champagne. It hurts."

"Drink lots of water today," Nadia advises her. "Okay, we're all here."

Carmine closes and locks the door. "I want to keep this between the six of us for a while. I don't think we need to involve the parents at this time."

"*You* don't have to be involved," Annika says. "Really, I can handle this."

"Can you?" Shane asks before I can. "Okay, what's your first move?"

"Nothing. I wait."

"Wrong," Shane replies. "We're going to question the staff. We're going to look at security disks. We're going to hunt these motherfuckers down and kill them."

"Can't I just sue them? Why do people have to die all the time?"

"Because they deserve it."

They deserve much more than just death.

And I'll be the one to hand it out.

"Nadia and Carmine are headed out on their honeymoon," Annika begins, but Nadia shakes her head.

"We're postponing, but only for a little while."

"No. No, Nadia. You deserve this break. Go on your honeymoon. I have these three looking out for me— whether I like it or not."

"Hey," Ivie says with a scowl, and I feel my lips twitch.

"Do you really think I'll just leave when this is going down?" Nadia demands. "Not a chance in hell. Besides, we'll get it wrapped up quickly, and I'll be lying on a tropical beach somewhere before I know it."

"I have a flight to catch this afternoon," Annika says, checking the time. "I'm headed back to Denver so I can get back to work."

"No."

She arches a brow at my one-word proclamation.

"Excuse me?"

"I didn't stutter. You're not taking a commercial flight."

She props her hands on her hips. "Yes, I am. I'm not like you. I don't always have to take a private jet."

"Someone is threatening you. That means you won't be on a commercial flight, Annika. When the time comes to go back to Denver, I'll fly you."

"The time is *today*," she stresses. "To. Day."

"God, you're stubborn." I push my hand through my hair and shake my head. "I'm not trying to control you or be an asshole here. I'm going to keep you safe, whether you like it or not."

"You're a caveman," she retorts.

Carmine smirks.

Shane coughs into his hand.

"Me, caveman." I thump my chest. "Me save you."

Annika just rolls her eyes.

"Ivie and I will get started on the security disks," Shane says and then smiles down at Ivie. "As soon as her head feels better."

"I need another donut." Before she can stand and retrieve it, Shane fetches it for her. "Thank you. I'll be good in a few minutes."

"I have a call in to the catering company to ask about the waiter who delivered the envelope," Carmine adds. "We'll get to the bottom of this."

"And what do I do in the meantime? Just sit around and wait?"

"You have your computer with you," Ivie points out.

261

"You can get caught up on charting, make calls to patients, that sort of thing."

Annika blows out a breath. "Fine. I'll be in my room, working."

She stomps out of the room, and I want to run after her. My room is next to hers, and I heard her crying all night.

It's a personal torture, knowing that she hurts, but I know she wouldn't welcome my comfort.

"If I'm going to hack into stuff, I need more coffee," Ivie says.

"No one said you had to hack anything," Shane says with a laugh. "We *own* the security footage."

"Well, where's the fun in that?"

I blink at her, then look at Nadia. "What am I missing?"

"Ivie's killer with a computer," Shane says proudly. "She can hack into anything."

"Well, that'll come in handy." I grin and grab three donuts and a full cup of coffee, then head for the door. "I'll be in *my* room, making calls and keeping an eye on Annika. Just let me know if you find anything. I'll do the same."

The others nod as I stride out of the office and head up the stairs to the bedrooms.

I know my grandmother's old home like the back of my hand. My brothers and I practically grew up here. Since she died, it feels like we've spent even more time here.

That would make Gram happy.

I stop by Annika's door and press my ear against the wood.

The water's running.

She's in the shower.

I walk into my space and shove a donut into my mouth while I boot up my computer.

YOU CAN ORDER Off the Record here: https://www.kristenprobyauthor.com/offtherecord

NEWSLETTER SIGN UP

I hope you enjoyed reading this story as much as I enjoyed writing it! For upcoming book news, be sure to join my newsletter! I promise I will only send you news-filled mail, and none of the spam. You can sign up here:

https://mailchi.mp/kristenproby.com/ newsletter-sign-up

ALSO BY KRISTEN PROBY:

Other Books by Kristen Proby

The With Me In Seattle Series

Come Away With Me
Under The Mistletoe With Me
Fight With Me
Play With Me
Rock With Me
Safe With Me
Tied With Me
Breathe With Me
Forever With Me
Stay With Me
Indulge With Me
Love With Me
Dance With Me

Honor
Courage

Check out the full Big Sky universe here: https://www.kristenprobyauthor.com/under-the-big-sky

Bayou Magic
Shadows
Spells

Check out the full series here: https://www.kristenprobyauthor.com/bayou-magic

The Romancing Manhattan Series

All the Way
All it Takes
After All

Check out the full series here: https://www.kristenprobyauthor.com/romancing-manhattan

The Boudreaux Series

Easy Love
Easy Charm
Easy Melody
Easy Kisses
Easy Magic

Easy Fortune

Easy Nights

Check out the full series here: https://www.
kristenprobyauthor.com/boudreaux

The Fusion Series

Listen to Me

Close to You

Blush for Me

The Beauty of Us

Savor You

Check out the full series here: https://www.
kristenprobyauthor.com/fusion

From 1001 Dark Nights

Easy With You

Easy For Keeps

No Reservations

Tempting Brooke

Wonder With Me

Shine With Me

Kristen Proby's Crossover Collection

Soaring with Fallon, A Big Sky Novel

Wicked Force: A Wicked Horse Vegas/Big Sky Novella
By Sawyer Bennett

All Stars Fall: A Seaside Pictures/Big Sky Novella
By Rachel Van Dyken

Hold On: A Play On/Big Sky Novella
By Samantha Young

Worth Fighting For: A Warrior Fight Club/Big Sky
Novella
By Laura Kaye

Crazy Imperfect Love: A Dirty Dicks/Big Sky Novella
By K.L. Grayson

Nothing Without You: A Forever Yours/Big Sky
Novella
By Monica Murphy

Check out the entire Crossover Collection here:
https://www.kristenprobyauthor.com/kristen-proby-
crossover-collection

ABOUT THE AUTHOR

Kristen Proby has published close to sixty titles, many of which have hit the USA Today, New York Times and Wall Street Journal Bestsellers lists. She continues to self publish, best known for her With Me In Seattle, Big Sky and Boudreaux series.

Kristen and her husband, John, make their home in her hometown of Whitefish, Montana with their two cats and French Bulldog named Rosie.

facebook.com/booksbykristenproby
instagram.com/kristenproby
bookbub.com/profile/kristen-proby
goodreads.com/kristenproby